TAKE ADVENTURE INTO YOUR OWN HANDS
WITH BOOKS BY BILL DOYLE!

Escape This Book! Titanic

Escape This Book! Tombs of Egypt

Escape This Book! Race to the Moon

THE FIFTH HERO

THE RACE TO ERASE

BILL DOYLE

Random House 🏠 New York

Text copyright © 2023 by Bill Doyle
Cover art copyright © 2023 by Antoine Losty
Logo lettering copyright © 2023 by Jacey

All rights reserved. Published in the United States by Random House Children's Books,
a division of Penguin Random House LLC, New York.

Random House and the colophon are registered trademarks of Penguin Random House LLC.

Visit us on the Web! rhcbooks.com

Educators and librarians, for a variety of teaching tools, visit us at RHTeachersLibrarians.com

Library of Congress Cataloging-in-Publication Data
Name: Doyle, Bill H., author.
Title: The race to erase / Bill Doyle.
Description: First edition. | New York: Random House Children's Books, [2023] |
Series: The fifth hero | Summary: Four kids with the power to speak to creatures, shake the
earth, manipulate water, and control the wind are on a mission to save the earth from the evil
Calamity Corporation—and readers must make a choice in three scenarios that change the
course of the adventure.
Identifiers: LCCN 2022012949 (print) | LCCN 2022012950 (ebook) |
ISBN 978-0-593-48637-5 (trade) | ISBN 978-0-593-48638-2 (lib. bdg.) |
ISBN 978-0-593-48639-9 (ebook)
Subjects: CYAC: Superheroes—Fiction. | Plot-your-own stories. | LCGFT: Superhero fiction. |
Choose-your-own stories.
Classification: LCC PZ7.D7725 Rab 2023 (print) | LCC PZ7.D7725 (ebook) |
DDC [Fic]—dc23

The text of this book is set in 12.25-point Adobe Garamond Pro.
Interior design by Jen Valero

Printed in the United States of America
10 9 8 7 6 5 4 3 2 1
First Edition

For caroline, thanks for the escape!

CHAPTER ONE

Vzzzt! Vzzt!

The timer on the handlebars buzzed, and Jarrett felt the unicycle lurch under his butt.

Uh-oh.

He could still make it to a transfer spot and switch to a new guzzler. But the nearest guzzler station was in the opposite direction, way back down the empty road. Besides, Lina's mansion must be nearby—or at least Jarrett hoped so. He didn't dare waste time checking his phone. He was dangerously close to being late for the Climate Club meeting and, more important, Lina's party for her eleventh birthday.

The guzzler's single tire started falling apart, like the tires always did after an hour of use. Bits of smoking rubber flew off, sizzling on the hot morning pavement. The burning smell made Jarrett's eyes water.

Time for a shortcut. He'd have to guzzle through the woods, which terrified him, but maybe the patchy grass would be softer on the fragile tire. Before he could overthink it, he veered off the road and bounced onto what looked like an animal path through the trees. A passing branch poked his arm just as the silver line of a security scanner ran over his body. He guessed he must be on Lina's property now.

Come on, guzzler, you can do it! he urged. *Just a little bit farther to the mansion. You can make it!*

Nope. No, it couldn't.

The last strips of smoking rubber peeled off the rim, leaving scorch marks on the leaf-covered path. The guzzler's metal wheel spun into the ground, like a giant pizza cutter, and got trapped between two rocks. The unicycle snapped back and then forward, shooting Jarrett over the handlebars and flipping him through the air.

Umph! Jarrett's body hit the ground. Luckily, his backpack cushioned the blow. Or unluckily, actually. The birthday presents inside had smashed, and as the bag burst open, plastic packing peanuts exploded around him. *Not good.* He lay there for a second before clambering to his feet. Of course, Jarrett didn't bother picking up the plastic peanuts as he resealed the backpack. He'd just leave them and the busted guzzler right where they were. Earth was old anyway, and other bits of garbage were already blowing among the trees nearby. What was a little more?

Hold on.

Those weren't bits of garbage bouncing here and there. They were . . . *chipmunks?*

Jarrett froze. A frightened gasp squeaked through his clamped lips, like a balloon leaking a five-second *pppptttt* of air. The chipmunks might have thought the high-pitched sound was him trying to communicate. They tilted their heads, listening, all the while their little jaws chewing away.

What were they chewing on?

Jarrett struggled to remember. Were chipmunks omnivores? Did they eat plants and . . .

People?

No, that's just silly, he told himself. Or was it? With so much wrong information out there, it was hard to know what was true anymore.

In a panic, Jarrett whipped around to get away and— *ooof!*—ran straight into a tree. He heard one of the chipmunks chittering like that was the funniest thing it had ever seen.

Jarrett brushed himself off, just in case a tree spider or another creepy bug had jumped on him. He hurried in what he hoped was the direction of the mansion. Above the treetops, birds swooped and shrieked. Were they vultures? And was that a moose (or a cow?) in the shadows back toward the road? And what was that *smell*?

This was why Jarrett was so glad he lived in a *city* like Oceanside. (Which, by the way, was nowhere near the ocean. A city planner had thought that name sounded better than Woodsy Flat Land.) In Oceanside he didn't have to deal with all these weird smells and terrifying animals.

Kind of like the creature crouching on a low tree branch about twenty feet ahead. *Wait a second!* Was that a mountain lion waiting to pounce on him?

Jarrett jerked to a stop. He thought about screaming for help. He thought about running for his life. And finally he thought *Ha!* when the "mountain lion" said:

"Yoo-hoo!"

Phew. The shadows had played tricks on Jarrett's eyes. It was just his best friend, Agnes, in a half crouch on the end of the branch. As always, her hair was spectacular. Long and black, with supertight curls that fell halfway to the waist of her white denim overalls. She pinwheeled her arms to keep her balance.

"Agnes!" he warned, suddenly in a panic again.

"What's wrong?" she said, mocking his urgent tone. "Do I have something in my teeth?"

"That branch!" he yelled. "It's going to break!"

"Relax." She smirked, bouncing on the branch. "How can you be in the Climate Club when you know so little about nature?"

"Um, you're not exactly a nature expert yourself," he shot back. "And you know why I'm in the Climate Club!"

"Yes, sure, to hang more with Malik and—"

Jarrett held up his hand to stop her from finishing. He was nervous enough already.

"Fine!" she cried dramatically. "But you've been missing out. Nature is like an amusement park, and this is just one of its rides!" With a wicked grin, she stood all the way up and bounced higher and lower. "Why would the tree have a branch if it wasn't totally safe?"

Finally, the branch made a snapping sound but didn't break. Instead, the end lowered to the ground. Agnes just stepped off, as if she'd planned all along for that to happen, leaving the bent branch dangling oddly behind her.

"See?" she asked smugly. "Let's go. Lina said her security scan spotted you, so I came to find you. The rest of the Climate Club is over there." When Jarrett started walking in the direction she'd pointed, Agnes got a look at his shorts. "Nice wardrobe choice. I heard grass stains are all the rage in Milan."

He laughed—it was hard not to. Agnes was constantly giving him a hard time but always in a funny way. Besides, Jarrett couldn't help it that he liked having the latest clothes. Today he was wearing lime-green shorts. The collar and sleeves of his red polo matched his shorts, and so did his backpack.

"Grass stains don't come out of clothes, do they?" he asked, stopping to rub at the dark green streaks on his shorts.

Agnes shrugged. "Probably not. Good thing clothes are disposable after one or two wears anyway."

That didn't ease his mind. "I like these shorts, that's all." After a pause, he added, "Lime green is kind of our favorite color."

"*Our?* You mean you and . . . ?"

"Fine, yes, Malik," he said, knowing he couldn't avoid the subject forever, especially since Malik was going to be at the meeting today too.

"Malik's great," Agnes said, "but style is not really important to him." She reached for Jarrett's hand and pulled him along. "Being your friend is his thing, though, I know it."

"I hope you're right." Jarrett's feet crunched on leaves and twigs as they walked—it felt weird, like stepping on little bones or something. That was another reason why being inside was way better. "I'm glad you're here, Aggie. I need the moral support."

"No problem, I've got you." Agnes let go of his hand to give his nose a playful **boop** with her finger. "I'll also protect you from Lina's rage for being late, Jar Jar."

But even her silly nickname for him couldn't get rid of the sudden feeling that things were about to go terribly wrong.

CHAPTER TWO

Jarrett and Agnes emerged from the trees onto a lawn of fake grass that spread out in a circle for acres. It was so fake and so green that it made Jarrett's eyes water again. In the center of the circle rose a mansion that resembled an airport . . . or an octopus. The middle of the mansion was a giant, shiny globe, maybe six stories high. Eight arms extended from the globe about two hundred yards in different directions. From these arms, car-sized FuelFlighter ships were taking off and landing constantly. Clearly, Lina's family ran much of its business from home.

With so much to check out, it took a second for Jarrett to spot the three other members of the Climate Club, standing in the shade closer to the mansion. They were hanging out next to a clump of tall bushes that had been clipped to look like a herd of dinosaurs.

"Finally!" Lina shouted at Jarrett and Agnes, waving them over impatiently. Lina wore black pants and a black T-shirt, her bald head shining even in the shade. She said she didn't like wasting time on washing and combing her hair. It was easier just to shave it clean with an electric razor every few days.

When Jarrett reached the little group, he gave Freya a double thumbs-up. Sure, it was a weird greeting, but he didn't really know her. Freya was the new girl at school this year. Jarrett's mom had told him that Freya was being raised by her grandparents. Before coming to Oceanside, they'd lived out west—just the three of them, alone in a big house without any neighbors. So that might be why Freya talked like an eighty-year-old from 1989. At first, she'd said things like "eat my shorts" and "bodacious." Then, when that met with nothing but giggles and confusion, she just stopped talking very much.

For some reason, she was all dressed up, wearing an aqua shirtdress with a heavy blue belt. She looked taller than usual. She had piled her long red hair on top of her head and was sporting ankle-high black boots. After Freya gave him a thumbs-up of her own, Jarret finally turned to Malik nervously. They hadn't seen each other outside school in a long time.

His friend—Malik and he *were* friends, right?—wore basketball shorts and a button-down shirt with a bow tie, and he was holding a black leather briefcase in one hand. He was dressed like a basketball-playing businessman, but somehow Malik still managed to look cool.

"Hey," Jarrett said. Malik gave the tiniest wave possible and then quickly looked away.

Ugh, that didn't go so great, Jarrett thought, and shared a look with Agnes.

"You're more than two minutes late, Jarrett," Lina sang in a fake, cheery voice while the tiny drones that filmed *The Lina Show* flew around them in a swirling cloud. "We need to talk about Climate Club, I guess, before we get to the important topic of the day . . . my birthday!" Then, noticing Jarrett's grass-stained shorts, she dropped the singsongy tone. "You didn't *walk* here, did you?"

Scoffing, Jarrett lied, "No, of course not."

"Oh, he totally walked here!" Agnes chimed in.

The drones froze as if someone had just burped at a funeral.

"Thanks, Agnes," Jarrett said through clenched teeth. So much for protecting him.

Agnes gave him a funny bow. As usual, whenever his friend did something goofy, he had to laugh.

"Okay, okay, Lina," he admitted. "My guzzler fell apart just inside your property. But I didn't walk that far."

Lina glanced at the drone nearest to her as if thinking about what this scene would look like to her millions of viewers. Suddenly, she became all soft and caring. "You should've just grabbed a new guzzler at a station. That's why my family provides them, after all. Sit down. Do you feel okay?"

But she didn't really do soft and caring, and watching her try was as creepy as spotting a hungry chipmunk.

"What? Yeah," Jarrett spluttered. "Actually, I feel fine."

Lina snapped her head back and forth. "No, you don't. You couldn't possibly. You, as the Climate Club servant must know that—"

"Secretary," he corrected her. "I'm the Climate Club secretary."

"—nobody should ever walk that far." Lina moved her fingers like she was casting a spell, and a chair zipped toward them across the lawn. Gesture cameras on the drones knew what she wanted just by the way she waved her hands. Lina had all the latest gadgets, mind-blowing tech that the public wouldn't be able to get for years. At school, she bragged constantly about the EyePhone, the contact-lens phone she wore in her eyes that let her text just by blinking.

Maybe Lina was right, Jarrett thought; maybe he didn't feel so hot. Maybe it was the way things were going with Malik, or maybe it was the walk after all. Everyone knew that walking outside was bad for you—and risky, with all the pollution, droughts, and floods.

"That's why it's so important people start listening to Climate Club's message," Lina was saying, more to the cameras than to the kids in front of her. "We need to get off Earth as soon as we can. This is a dangerous planet! More people need to listen to my parents . . . and to *me.*"

Blech. This was just another chance for Lina to make everything about her. Jarrett didn't feel like being part of her show today. He flicked the chair away with a motion of his hand. But he must have made the wrong gesture, because the chair shot straight up into the air and flew out of sight.

Lina blinked and leaned in close to Jarrett so she could angry-whisper, "Remember our deal? You get to be in the Climate Club, but you have to smile for the cameras, please." Then, more loudly so the drones could hear her, "That's the reason my family's company makes guzzlers available to everyone everywhere. So no one has to walk or run outside. Oh, sorry, did you guys know my family makes guzzlers?"

She smiled to let them know she was joking. Of course they knew her family made the guzzlers. The same way they knew her family made disposable cars and planes, and gigantic houses and hotels . . . both on Earth and in outer space.

With a clap of her hands, Lina announced, "That's enough Climate Club for the day. Let's get my birthday party started. Follow me!"

Lina led them to the main entrance of the mansion and through tall doors that Jarrett guessed were at least three stories high. Everything glittered, from the shining marble floor with *CC*, for Calamity Corporation, painted in gold to the sparkling overhead chandeliers.

"Whoa, it's all so . . . new," Agnes breathed, her fingers leaving tracks in the thick velvet wallpaper. "Did you just move in?"

"No, we redecorate twice a month," Lina said. "Got to keep up with the trends! Can't have Mom's new blue shoes clashing with the sofa, right?" She laughed. "And as long as the sofa is going, why not redecorate the entire place? All one hundred thirty-five rooms of it."

The gentle hum of air-conditioning, the light plinking of harp music, the soft carpet under his feet—this house was so different from Jarrett's family's apartment. His parents and he and his five brothers and sisters lived in a two-bedroom place with bunk beds and a pullout couch in the living room. It was so noisy and crowded that Jarrett had turned his lower bunk into a blanket-covered fort to escape the chaos.

But here at Lina's, everything was in order. Silent high-speed escalators whisked the kids up to the fifth floor. There they were greeted by shouting voices and strange singing. Jarrett quickly spotted the source. Large video screens lined both walls down a long hallway.

Dramatic music and slogans pumped out of speakers and filled the air. One screen showed a forest fire while a Holly-wood actor said in a low voice, "A good winner knows when they've lost. It's time to give up on Earth. It's time to start winning again . . . up in space." Another screen had pictures of hotels that orbited Earth, with the words *Let's Zoom from the Doom to Your Room Above the Gloom.*

Lina gestured toward the yammering, flashing screens. "My parents put their favorite ads for the company up here. I'm kind of sick of them, to tell you the truth. Let me figure out how to turn them off." She kept moving on down the hallway and disappeared around the corner. The other kids had stopped, though, drawn to the ad for the latest *Race to Erase.*

Every month the Calamity Corporation held a new Race to Erase. Each race had a different goal or target, but it was always something horrible on Earth to erase. The last race's target had been poison ivy, and before that it had been bloodsucking leeches. To win the race, teams tried to destroy or capture more than any other team. The grand prize was always a rocket to tour the new space communities being built by the Calamity Corporation.

"Are you up for the next Race to Erase challenge?" the ad shouted. "Prove it! This time you'll have to capture bats! Sound easy? Hold on. You'll have to catch these specific bats!" An image of what looked like a long-nosed rat with hairy black wings popped up on the screen.

"Ew," Jarrett said, stepping back.

"Not ew," Agnes said. "Cool."

"These lesser long-nosed bats are nocturnal," the ad continued. "That means you'll need to hunt down their daytime nests if you want to catch them. And guess what! They're almost extinct! Get to the finish line in the Chihuahuan Desert, New Mexico, before the last rays of the sun disappear over the horizon with more bats than any other competitor, and you win! The competition starts in just one hour, so get ready to Race to Erase!"

Jarrett squirmed. He couldn't imagine why anyone would ever enter a race like that. He didn't care what the prize was. Bats were disgusting.

More voices drifted out from the darkness of a nearby room. "Come on, better catch up with Lina," Malik said. But, as they stepped into the shadows just inside the room, it was obvious Lina wasn't there.

Instead, Jarrett recognized projections of Lina's parents, Dr. and Dr. Limwick, standing on a small stage at the far side of the room. Their outlines glowed, a dead giveaway that they were holograms. In between the kids and the stage was a high-back command chair turned away from them. Almost like a throne, it sat in front of a large control panel. Jarrett could make out the top of a curly-haired head over the back of the chair, and below he could see toes just barely touching the ground.

Was that Tommy? Lina's older brother was a senior in high school. Before Jarrett could say anything, Freya pulled him back, deeper into the shadows near the door.

"The Race to Erase is today, darling," Lina's mom was saying. "Let's just focus on that, Tommy."

Aha! Jarrett thought. So it *was* Tommy sitting in the chair.

"Even if we had a thousand races over the next ten years," Tommy moaned, "we could cause more damage in just one day with the Ponies!"

Jarrett didn't want to eavesdrop. He tried gently pushing Freya and the others back out to the hallway, but Freya wouldn't move.

"Honey, we talked about this," Tommy's dad said.

"You guys aren't listening to me!" Tommy fired back.

Whoa. Jarrett could only imagine his parents' reaction if

he used that tone with them. It would not be pretty. But Tommy's mom just nodded patiently and said, "All right, darling, we're listening. Tell us again what you're thinking."

"Okay, gee, thanks so much," Tommy said peevishly. Then, after a breath, he said more politely, "It's time for us to take action once and for all."

"And we are, Tommy," his dad assured him. "We want—"

"Listen to me," Tommy interrupted.

He waited to be sure his parents were listening before he finally said:

"It's time to mortally wound the planet."

CHAPTER THREE

Jarrett shook his head to clear his ears.

Mortally wound the planet?

He felt Freya tense next to him. He glanced at the others; Agnes's eyes were wide with surprise, and Malik was looking toward the way out. Jarrett was suddenly very happy Tommy hadn't noticed them yet.

"Darling, shhh," his mom chided. "We don't say things like that. At least not out loud."

"And certainly not in emails or texts," his dad added with a chuckle.

"I'm serious, you guys," Tommy said. "Now's the time to use my top-secret project. The Four Powerful Obliteration of Natural Existence Spheres."

"Yes, yes," his mom said. "The Four Ponies for short. That's the most adorable name, darling."

"I came up with that!" Tommy said. "When we drop the spheres from space, the Four Ponies will become part of whatever they touch first on Earth."

"That's right," his mom said. "You have four spheres, one for animals, one for water, one for land, and . . ." She glanced at his dad, as if asking if he knew what the next one was.

"Air, Mom!" Tommy shouted. "How can you guys not remember? Animals. Water. Land. And air. The spheres' artificial intelligence will all work together to make those elements so powerful that Earth will become unlivable. This is really important to me—and the future of the company!"

"But your Ponies need more testing," his mom said calmly. "Those little spheres cost more than a trillion dollars, dear. And we really don't know what will happen when they're absorbed by the elements."

"Your mother's right," his dad chimed in. "Don't forget, Tommy, that humans are animals. We don't want the spheres damaging our customers, do we? No, it sounds far too dangerous, even for us."

Then he added with another chuckle, "And you know how we love a good calamity."

Alarms on both doctors' wrists beeped once.

"That means we have thirty more seconds in our schedules for 'time with son,'" Tommy's dad said. "Let's talk about today."

"Yes, let's," his mom agreed. "We'll come down at the end of the Race to Erase to award the winning team before taking off again."

But Tommy wasn't interested in changing the subject. "Who cares about the race?"

"Tommy, twenty-five seconds left," his mom warned.

"Okay, sure." Tommy's words sped up. "The spheres will destroy a ton of species. But Calamity Corporation can make robots to take their place. That means robots of all the animals, like bears and lions, and little ones like gophers and scorpions—"

Freya gasped. Not the best time to stop being the strong, silent type. She slapped her hand to her mouth to keep from making any other sounds. Too late.

"Who's there?" Tommy spun his chair around so he was facing the door and the kids . . . but they were safely tucked into the shadows. "It's nothing," he said, and swung the chair back toward his parents. "I've put the Four Ponies in the pink FuelFlighter as a surprise for you. . . . Mom? Dad?"

But Tommy's parents were gone—their holograms had blipped out while he was looking away. Before they disappeared, Jarrett thought he heard them say, "We love you."

Silently, Jarrett turned to Freya and this time gave a determined push. He herded her, Malik, and Agnes out of the room before Tommy could spot them. They stumbled into the hall just as Tommy muttered, "Thanks, Mom and Dad. I'll take that as a yes."

The long hallway was quiet; Lina must have turned off the ads. There was just the sound of a drone vacuuming in a faraway room. The four kids stared at each other with wide eyes.

Agnes whispered, "Was that a joke about Earth? I mean, they wouldn't actually do all that stuff. . . ."

"No way," Jarrett whispered back. "Over just the past year, the Calamity Corporation has saved the world from"—he ticked items off on his fingers—"a global flood, a planetary drought, two mega hurricanes, and five maximum earthquakes!"

This seemed to calm Agnes down. "You're right. Lina's family tries to save the world, not destroy it. Plus, they pay for Climate Club stuff like snacks at meetings." Still not really convinced, she turned to Freya. "What do you think?"

"Not sure; can I get back to you later?" Freya answered. When she didn't talk like she was eighty, she spoke like the automatic responses people sent in text messages.

"Um, okay . . . ," Agnes said. "Malik, what do you say?"

Malik looked more impatient than scared. "So, are Lina's

parents here or not? Or were they hologramming from far away?"

Crossing her arms, Freya glared at him, and Agnes said, "That's what you care about? Meeting her parents? Didn't you hear what they were just saying?"

"What does it matter?" Malik shot back. "Their mom and dad told Tommy to chill out and not do anything."

"Hey!"

The four jumped at the sound of Lina's voice. She marched toward them down the hall, the swarm of camera drones buzzing around her. Eager to put distance between themselves and Tommy, Jarrett and the others rushed to meet her halfway.

"What are you guys doing?" Lina demanded, jerking her chin toward Tommy's room. "That's not part of my birthday plan. That's just what my brother calls his secret laboratory. Like an evil scientist. Totally on brand for him."

"Hey, Lina," Malik said. "Where are your parents?"

Lina blinked at the randomness of the question. "They're off world, working on a space hotel. Why?"

"No big deal, just my mom and dad want me to talk to—"

"Don't be boring, Malik. Everyone wants to talk to my parents," Lina interrupted. "Did you see them holo-calling Tommy? What were they talking about?"

"The pink FuelFlighter—" Jarrett started, and then closed his mouth. He knew that Lina wouldn't like that they had overheard Tommy's plan. And what had they heard anyway? Tommy must have been joking. To change the subject, Jarrett pointed down at the beige carpet. "This is gorgeous!"

"Um, all right, weirdo," Lina said, not buying his sudden interest in the carpet. "What about the pink FF?"

"We can't tell you!" Agnes blurted. "It's a surprise!"

"A surprise for me?" Lina looked doubtful, but hopeful. "I don't get surprises from my family."

The others must have looked shocked, because Lina explained, "My parents say I can have everything I want whenever I want it, so why would I need surprises on my birthday?"

Jarrett thought surprises could be the best parts of birthdays. Like the time his whole family waited until he came out of school and sang "Happy Birthday" at the top of their lungs.

"I don't know, Lina," Agnes said, still acting. "Maybe your parents are going to surprise you with a surprise gift!"

"Maybe," Lina said, and then seemed to toss out the idea. "But surely they can't be the only ones who might have a gift for me. . . ." She waggled her eyebrows at them.

Oh right, Jarrett thought. "Time for the presents?"

"Well, if you insist," Lina said, plopping down on a nearby oversize chair. She rested her elbows on the arms of the seat and steepled her fingers. The queen was waiting for gifts.

Agnes guffawed. "Seriously? You have everything, Lina. No one knows what present to get you, and everyone is scared to try!"

Good point, Jarrett thought. That fear—combined with Lina's prickly personality—was probably why no other kids had showed up today. Lina had invited their whole class, but only Agnes, Freya, Malik, and Jarrett had said yes. Mostly because Lina had made it an official Climate Club meeting, so they had to come.

Lina somehow kept her tight smile for the swirling cameras. "Thanks for the gift of nothing, Agnes!" She turned her attention to Freya. "And what did you bring?"

For a second, Freya just stared back at Lina.

"Who, me?" she finally said. "I brought what Agnes brought."

Lina's eyes bulged. "Nothing is a very popular gift."

Not for the first time, Jarrett wondered why Freya was here. Why would she put up with that guff from Lina? Malik had joined the Climate Club because his family made elevators for space hotels. His parents wanted him to get closer to Lina so her family would buy the elevators. And Jarrett had joined to hang out with Malik. Agnes was here to support Jarrett. But Freya was a mystery. . . . Why had she joined Climate Club?

Malik stepped in front of Lina and reached into his briefcase. "I'll bet your parents will want to see what I brought you!" He pulled out a bag filled with dirty gray water and something solid in the center.

"It's flowering coral," Malik said uncertainly. A dead fish had jostled free and now floated upside down at the top of the water. "Huh, it was beautiful when I took it out of the ocean yesterday."

Clearly struggling to keep her temper, Lina looked at Jarrett. "What did you bring? Or do you need to use one of the gift-wrapping rooms?"

Jarrett didn't even bother reaching into his backpack. His smashed gifts seemed dumb now. He shook his head and gazed at the carpet again.

"No one brought anything else?" Lina's fake smile dipped. "This is the best party ever!"

"Hooray!" Agnes cried, adding to Lina's sarcasm. "Surprise!"

Lina rolled her eyes, but then her smile grew again. "Actually, that's a great idea!"

Somehow this new smile seemed more alarming than

anything else that day. "What are you thinking?" Jarrett asked nervously.

Lina waved her hands, and the drones filming them went dark and plunged to the carpet with tiny thuds.

Jarrett couldn't believe it. "No more *Lina Show*?"

"Oh, it's always *The Lina Show*," Lina said, chuckling. "But I'm ready for a real surprise. Let's see what my family got me. You said it's in the pink FuelFlighter, right?"

Not waiting for an answer, she hopped to her feet and guided them to the center of the hall. Once they were in a single-file line, she gestured in the air, and the section of carpet beneath their feet began to move slowly. Lina waved her hands again, and they picked up speed. Soon they were zipping through the length of the house, almost like riding a magic carpet. In moments they arrived at the small hangar of a pink FuelFlighter. A wheeled delivery robot was just rolling out of the ship's open hatch.

"My surprise must be inside," Lina guessed, and hurried the little group on board. "You people are about to learn what it means to give a real gift!"

The ship could hold twelve passengers on the plush leather couches that lined the walls, so there was plenty of room for the five of them. Their shoes squeaked on the thick glass floor that allowed passengers to gaze down at Earth from space. Jarrett just noticed the control panel in the center of the ship was dim when—

The hatch slid shut behind them, and the FF's engines fired. It jerked up from the launchpad.

The sudden force knocked Jarrett and Freya onto couches, and the others were tossed sprawling on the floor. Through the glass bottom of the FF, Jarrett could see the ground falling away beneath them as the ship shot into the air.

As the mansion below got smaller, Jarrett had to look away from the windows. The view was making him too dizzy. He got unsteadily to his feet, and so did the others. Lina went to the other side of the control panel, so she faced them.

"Maybe a little warning next time, Lina?" Malik said.

"Let's go faster!" Agnes shouted, loving the unexpected takeoff. But as they rose higher and higher, Jarrett could feel something wasn't right.

"Isn't this the best?" Lina's smile was bigger—and faker—than ever. "This must all be part of my surprise." Her hands flew over the dim control panel. But it reminded Jarrett of the Super Bowl halftime show when musicians only pretended to play instruments.

"Uh, Lina?" he said.

"What, Jarrett? I'm kind of busy flying over here." Lina poked at a few buttons as if to prove it.

"Really?" Jarrett was scared to ask, but he had to know. "Are you driving this thing?"

"Of course," Lina said. But then she seemed to think, why bother lying? She held her hands up, away from the panel, and looked Jarrett in the eyes.

"Okay, smart guy, you got me," she said. "I have no idea what's happening. This ship is totally out of control."

CHAPTER FOUR

Earth continued to get smaller beneath them. And the FuelFlighter's blasting engines showed no sign of slowing down. As the ship hit a pocket of air and sent the kids stumbling, Jarrett had another scary thought. "Are we headed to the moon or something, Lina?"

Lina blew out air as if the question were ridiculous. "This is a FuelFlighter, not a planetary rocket."

That didn't soothe Jarrett's nerves. "So, is that a no?"

Her answer was a shrug. Her face glowed from the dim light of the screens on the panel.

"What about air? And food?" Malik demanded. "Do we have enough to get to wherever we're going?"

Finally Lina looked up and ordered, "Relax, people."

"Relax?" Jarrett blurted. "How can we relax?"

"It looks like this FF is on a mission," Lina said, tapping one of the screens on the control panel. "But I don't know what that is. Once its mission is over, the autopilot will turn off and I'll be able to take control."

"Can you call for help?" Malik asked.

Lina shook her head. "Nope, the radio isn't working. And my EyePhone is out of range."

Freya was the first to check her own phone, and then they all did. "We're out of range too," Agnes said.

"But there's no reason to call anyone!" Lina sounded fed up. "You said my parents set up a surprise as my birthday present. This must just be a fun sightseeing mission for the Climate Club."

"Um." Agnes ran a hand through her curls. "We might have exaggerated a bit when we said you a had surprise waiting in here. Sorry."

As that sank in, Lina's shoulders sagged a little. Then she shrugged and gave Agnes a little smile. "I don't know. I'm pretty surprised."

Humming got Jarrett's attention. It was coming from Freya, who was standing in the center of the ship, looking down through the window. Seeing her thick, hard boots on the clear surface was enough to make Jarrett want to scream.

"Um, Freya," he said, trying to stay calm. "Do you think you should be standing on glass in those boots?"

Her face came up and now he could hear a little better what she was singing. It was soft. *Just look down. From up here it doesn't look so bad.*"

Jarrett forced himself to look down again and saw that she was right. Yes, it was dizzying but also incredible. They had always heard how horrible Earth was. But right now it looked beautiful. And fragile.

He opened his mouth to agree with Freya but was interrupted by four sharp sounds—**phick phick phick phick.** Four compartment doors had slid open on the wall across from Jarrett. Inside each one was a ball, just a little smaller than a golf ball. A track shot out from each compartment and extended to small, closed portals in the floor.

"Lina?" Jarrett asked. "Did you do that?"

Flicking random switches on the dim control panel, she shook her head. "I still can't do anything."

As all five kids watched with growing worry, the spheres started to glow with horrible, swirling colors. One was shocking red with flecks of yellow. Another was blue with squirming stripes of silver. The third was a green-brown that reminded Jarrett of an old sandwich he'd left in his school locker over summer break. And the last was a violet so intense, it made him feel like throwing up. His stomach churned.

"What are those?" Agnes said, sounding kind of sick too. "Some kind of spheres?"

"Wait, *spheres*?" That word struck Jarrett as important. "Are these the Four Ponies Tommy was talking about?"

Lina went pale. "The Ponies?" Her voice was thick with fear. "Those can't be the Ponies!"

"We should have told you," Agnes said to her. "Tommy put them in here for your parents. We didn't think he was serious. Or at least we hoped he wasn't."

"What? Why didn't you say something?" Lina demanded, looking horrified. "Stay away from the Ponies. Don't touch them! They have minds of their own!"

Taking a step back, Malik asked, "You think those tiny spheres could destroy the planet?"

"I'm not sure . . . ," Lina said. "What else do you know?"

"Tommy didn't say *destroy*," Malik told her. "But he did say *wound*."

"Your brother can't drop these," Agnes insisted. "Your parents told him not to!"

"Tommy doesn't always listen to Mom and Dad," Lina said. "But, good news, that must be the mission this Fuel-Flighter is on!"

Jarrett shook his head. "Good news?"

"Once the spheres roll down those tracks and out of the

FF, the mission will be done," Lina explained. "I'll be able to take control of the ship."

"Tommy said they would wipe out entire species, and humans are a species!" Agnes shouted. "That is *not* good news!"

My family is down there, Jarrett thought. *My friends are down there.*

As if reading his mind, Freya said, "The whole world is down there."

Lina looked at them. She was speechless. And that was the scariest part.

With more *phick*s of machinery, the Four Ponies were released from their compartments and started rolling smoothly and slowly down their tracks. The small circular portals at the bottom of each track opened, and icy wind blasted into the cabin. In no more than two seconds the balls would roll out of the ship.

Tommy's words flew into Jarrett's head. *It's time to mortally wound the planet.*

Without thinking, Jarrett snatched the sphere closest to him off its track. As he did, he could see Agnes, Malik, and Freya reach for the other spheres. An explosion of light partially blinded Jarrett, and a terrifying howling sound filled his ears.

He could barely make out Lina rushing around the

control panel toward them, her arms waving. "No! What are you doing?"

There was another flash of light. Jarrett felt a sharp pain as the sphere in his hand burned into his flesh.

The FuelFlighter lost power, and suddenly they were falling through the sky. Jarrett's palm sizzled, and he felt dizzier than ever. Stumbling, he reached out for support. He grabbed Freya's and Agnes's hands just as Agnes reached for Malik.

As Jarrett passed out, Lina shouted, "What are—"

QUICK! TURN TO PAGE 177!

CHAPTER SIX

"**Y**ou!"

Someone was yelling and shaking Jarrett awake. He opened his eyes. Where was he? Still falling from the sky in the FuelFighter?

No. He was on Lina's fake lawn, sprawled on his back with his head turned away from the mansion.

For some reason, the words *bath* and *choice* rang in his mind like a loud gong. Had someone made a choice of some kind? His brain fought to catch up. What was happening?

Around him, Malik, Agnes, and Freya were on their backs in the dirt, still knocked out.

"What?" Jarrett started to say, and finally swiveled his

head to look up. Tommy was standing over him, shaking him. He stopped when he saw Jarrett's open eyes.

"Finally, you're awake," Tommy grunted.

Somehow Lina had gotten them all back to Earth and out of the FF. And now she was holding a garden hose in her hand, with the sprayer pointed at Jarrett. She kept pulling the trigger on the sprayer, but it just made an empty clicking sound without producing a single drop of water. Had she been trying to wake him up with a splash of water before Tommy arrived? How long had she been doing that?

"Stupid thing." Lina shook the hose as if angry it wasn't doing her bidding, and then threw it onto the ground. The forest around them was dead. *How can that be?* Jarrett wondered. It had been green and filled with life just minutes ago. Had the *choice* about the *bath* had something to do with this? Was that why everything was so dry?

Scoffing, Lina said, "There's never water in the well when you need it."

"Another drought," Tommy crowed happily. "Even our family, the most powerful people on the planet, can't save Earth. And why would we want to? This planet is so *old*!"

"What's happening?" Jarrett finally managed. His hand burned. He held it in front of his face. Somehow, one of the Ponies was embedded under his skin. He tapped the hard, dark sphere with a finger of his other hand. "What is this?"

"That is something very special," Tommy said. "And you're going to give it back."

That didn't sound good. "Give it back? How?"

"Don't worry," Tommy said with half-hearted concern. "We'll put you to sleep before we take it out."

With that, Tommy helped Jarrett to his feet and started guiding him toward the mansion. "I'll send the big drones to pick up the other kids," Tommy told Lina over his shoulder.

Choice . . . choice . . . For some reason the word continued running through Jarrett's mind, almost like the wailing of a police siren, as he walked with Tommy.

Why was Jarrett hearing that word? And with such a strange effect, almost like four people talking at once.

Is there a choice I could have made differently? Jarrett wondered.

Or maybe someone else had made a decision recently? If only that person could go back to that last decision and make a different choice . . .

THE END

YOU CAN STILL SAVE THE DAY!
GO TO PAGE 177 AND TRY AGAIN.

CHAPTER SIX

" **Y**ou!"

A drop of water hit Jarrett's forehead, and even though he was passed out, it triggered a memory from a few weeks ago. Scenes played in his brain, all in that instant between sleeping and waking up.

In a flash, Jarrett was remembering Jarma.

Jarrett had been in science class, and Mr. Price had just instructed the students to pair up to work on a new project. Normally Jarrett would have gone straight to Agnes, but this day he turned to Malik instead. And he found that Malik was already looking at him.

"Hey, wanna . . . ?" Jarrett asked shakily. Why was he suddenly nervous? He'd known Malik since first grade.

"Sounds good, partner," Malik said, his face going red.

Mr. Price explained that each pair of students was required to care for an uncooked egg for a whole week. Jarrett missed the reason for the assignment. Maybe they were supposed to learn the fragility of life? He was too flustered to pay attention.

Some kids just tucked their eggs in their lockers and forgot about them. Others, like Agnes, dropped them the first day. Not Malik and Jarrett. Within minutes they had named their egg Jarma, using the first parts of their names, Jar and Ma. They decided they'd keep Jarma at Malik's house the first night, and then at Jarrett's the second, and they'd keep switching nights after that.

During school, they moved Malik's books, gym sneakers, and Detroit Lions football sweatshirt into Jarrett's locker. That way Jarma could have his own locker, a nest all to himself. The boys printed photos of themselves so Jarma had naptime with pictures of his dads around him. Then they started pretending Jarma was sending them both messages. Notes would appear in their backpacks as if Jarma were writing them. At first the notes had goofy puns, like the one Jarrett found before math class. It said, *It's no yoke, I think you're egg-ceptional.* Then the notes were simpler, like the two Malik found in science class. They read, *I miss you!* and *Hope the quiz went great!*

On the last evening of the egg assignment, the boys were heading to Malik's house on guzzlers. Malik had had an idea the day before to invent a new game by combining two sports, one that would work in smaller rooms of spaceships when everyone escaped Earth. They had played golf mashed up with basketball. They'd put Jarma safely off to the side with two little cotton balls in front of him. Those were his pom-poms so he could be their cheerleader.

Now, as they sped toward Malik's house, Malik was telling Jarrett about his latest idea of mashing up Ping-Pong with tackle football. The mist in the air had become a light rain. The water dripped onto Jarrett's forehead (just like the drop of water that triggered this whole memory), but he didn't even really notice it. He was too busy trying to balance on the guzzler one-handed. His other arm was between him and Malik's guzzler. That was where Malik and Jarrett each kept a hand on little Jarma as they sped along with their egg in the middle.

"What are you boys doing?" Malik's mom demanded from the porch as they pulled into Malik's driveway. Surprised, they jerked their hands apart and Jarma fell onto the wet pavement of the driveway, smashing. *We were so close,* Jarrett thought. The next day they would have returned Jarma safely to Mr. Price. But not anymore.

The palm of Jarrett's hand burned where he'd been

holding Jarma. Still up on the porch, Malik's mom said, "I think you boys have been hanging out together too much. Malik, I know you have other friends who must feel ignored, like Lina. Why not spend time with her and her family? Your father and I would love that. They need our elevators for all their new projects, don't they? I don't want you and Jarrett . . . seeing . . . each other on your own. At least for a bit."

Malik wouldn't look at Jarrett. "Okay, Mom."

Not sure what else to do, Jarrett pedaled home, leaving the shells of Jarma on the driveway in the now-pouring rain.

That week, Malik moved his stuff back to his own locker, and the school switched Mr. Price from teaching science to working as a receptionist in the principal's office. The new teacher, Mr. Podeszwa, announced they would be redoing the egg experiment. He gave the class hard-boiled eggs—not raw ones. He assigned Malik and Jarrett new partners and told everyone not to worry so much about taking care of the egg. It was just an egg, after all. There were always more.

Had it been the new teacher's idea to give them different partners, or had Malik asked for a new one?

The question had been eating at Jarrett ever since. Why had Malik stopped—?

A spray of cold water jolted Jarrett awake and out of his dream.

"That was the best birthday party, guys!" Lina was saying. "Okay, now that you've woken up from your . . . *naps* . . . time to go home."

Jarrett gasped and opened his eyes. He was sprawled on his back on Lina's front lawn. She was sitting in a lawn chair, squirting him with a garden hose. The water was freezing.

"Knock it off!" Jarrett sputtered.

He looked around. Malik, Agnes, and Freya were on their backs, too, sitting up and opening their eyes, their hair wet from when Lina must have sprayed them. Jarrett's hand felt like he'd just touched a hot stove. He examined it. There was just a hint of a circle on his palm, like the very top of a golf ball was under the skin, but otherwise it looked fine.

"What happened?" he demanded.

"You were napping," Lina told him.

When he just stared at her with an *Oh, come off it* look, she switched gears. "Okay, fine. We're telling the truth? You want to know *what happened*? Would that be before or after you grabbed on to the trillion-dollar spheres that are now absorbed into your bodies?" Lina didn't wait for an answer. "After *you* did that, *I* got control of the FF, brought us down safely, and dumped you guys out of the ship."

Jarrett shook his head. "You did what to us?"

Taking a breath, she calmed herself. "Very gently, don't worry. I just turned the FF on its side and kind of shook it up and down until you fell out of the hatch. You're fine. Don't be such a baby. I put the pink FF back in the dock."

"Super-fun party," Agnes commented, moving her legs so she was seated cross-legged. She peeled a patch of fake grass off her face from where her cheek had pressed into the ground.

Apparently, only Lina was allowed to use sarcasm. "No one asked you to save the world," she snapped. "No one asked you to grab the Four Ponies. What are the four of you now? Like, the Four Heroes of Planet Earth?"

Zip, zing. There was the chime just before a hologram appeared. As if knowing what was coming, Lina threw herself onto the ground.

"What—?" Agnes started to say.

Lina raised a hand to silence her as Tommy's glowing hologram image popped into the air just a few feet away. His shoes hovered about six inches off the ground, and he glared at them.

"What happened? Where are they?" Tommy shouted at Lina.

"Hey there, Tommy," Lina said, all calm and casual. "Where are what, big brother?"

Tommy's eyes darted around their group. "Why are you guys hanging around *outside,* acting all weird?"

"We're not acting weird." Lina shrugged. "We were just sitting here." She glanced at the others for help.

Freya chimed in, "Yes, we're just playing Hose. My grandparents showed it to me."

"Hose?" Tommy asked suspiciously.

"Yes, Hose," Agnes said, picking up on the idea. As if to show him how to play, she grabbed the hose from Lina and sprayed Jarrett.

"Hey!" Jarrett shouted.

"That's not helpful, just strange," Tommy said.

"Okay, bye!" Lina said, trying to get him to go. "Good luck finding them!" Then, to cover, "I mean, good luck finding whatever *they* are!"

Maybe Tommy was too distracted to notice her strange behavior. "I'll put Slicer and Dicer on it," he said. "They'll sniff them out."

Lina's fake smile dipped. "Wait," she said. "Would Mom and Dad be okay with that? Aren't they up in space? Like, eating space junk and smashing asteroids?"

"Your mom and dad eat space junk?" Freya asked.

"No, keep up," Lina answered. "Slicer and Dicer are robots. Our company uses them to destroy old satellites or meteors that get too close to Earth."

Not really listening, Tommy was nodding to himself. "It

will take Slicer and Dicer an hour to get on track, but they'll find the four things I'm looking for soon enough. I've got to go."

"Bye." Freya raised her hand with the orb in it to wave, and Lina slapped it down before Tommy could see it.

"Hey!" Freya protested. "That hurt!"

Laughing too loud, Lina explained to Tommy, "Just another fun game we play. Slap Hands."

Tommy just rolled his eyes, almost exactly the way Lina did. And blipped out.

"Sorry," Lina told Freya once his hologram was gone. "I panicked a little."

"Lina, just tell Tommy what happened!" Jarrett said.

"I can't. My family would never trust me again. And I like the 'everything' that comes with that trust. Plus, you are in troub—"

"What are these things?" Freya interrupted, tapping the little half bubble in her palm with a fingernail. There was a small, hollow sound. The orbs weren't glowing anymore but shone flatly, like dead eyes in the center of their palms.

"Mine's stuck in there," Malik said, tapping the orb in his hand.

"Shhh! Stop doing that!" Lina hissed as if they had just banged cymbals together. "We need to get you out of here.

We need an excuse for you to run away from Oceanside. But what . . . ?"

She touched her forehead for a second, thinking, then, "I got it! You're entering the race. Use your phones to tell your families you'll be home after dinner."

They reached for their phones, and all found the same thing; their screens were cracked, and the phones wouldn't even power on. "They must have gotten fried when we grabbed the orbs," Agnes said.

Without hesitating, Lina's eyes went off to the side, and Jarrett could see her typing by blinking. "I'm using my Eye-Phone to message your families right now. I'm letting them know you'll be busy with the competition and not to expect you home until after dinner. I should be able to figure things out by then."

"We can't enter the race!" Jarrett protested. "Look at us! Do we look like bat trappers to you?"

Lina nodded. "Of course not. That's just the excuse. I need time to figure out how to get those spheres out of your hands. Or do you want Slicer and Dicer to do the job?"

"Would we get to meet them?" Malik asked. "Space robots sound kind of cool."

Lina squinted at him like he was the most ridiculous creature she'd ever seen. "Oh, you want to meet them, do you?"

She blinked and gestured with both hands, tossing a hologram in front of the kids. The image must have been coming from a satellite orbiting Earth. The hologram showed two objects falling through the atmosphere toward Earth, a trail of flames behind them.

"That's Slicer"—she pointed at one of the shapes, and then at the other—"and that's Dicer."

Creepy, Jarrett thought, *but also kind of awesome.* They were like comets streaking through the sky.

"You guys," Lina breathed, frustrated. Apparently, she wasn't getting the reaction she wanted. "Let me zoom in."

She gestured again at the hologram, and the two shapes were magnified. Now details of the robots were clearer. They were each the size of two stacked superstore shopping carts. Not huge but way bigger than any of the kids.

"Do they have swords for arms?" Agnes asked, her voice cracking. Jarrett had never heard her sound nervous before.

Giving her shoulder a comforting pat, Jarrett peered more closely at the image. Yes, Agnes was right. The twin robots didn't have regular arms. Instead, attached to their shoulders were two sharp-looking blades that must have been about four feet long. That was when Jarrett spotted the only difference between the robots: Slicer's blades cut horizontally, and Dicer's blades cut vertically.

But the blades for arms weren't the scariest part about the

robots. It was their faces. Their gaping mouths were the size of open ovens and lined with pointy metal fangs. Their eyes bulged slightly out of their sockets as if the robots were enraged by *everything* they were seeing. And there was no light in their eyes. Zero. Even red would have been less scary than that pure darkness.

Alone each robot appeared deadly; together they looked . . . *What's the next step beyond deadly?* Jarrett wondered, and realized he definitely didn't want to find out.

Sounding satisfied that she finally had their attention, Lina said, "These robots are designed to slice and dice asteroids the size of New York City and cut up space junk in just seconds. What do you think will happen when they find out the Ponies are stuck in your hands?"

The others were too stunned to respond, and Lina asked, "Any questions?"

"Yes, I've got a question," Freya finally said quietly. "Why aren't we running? I mean, right now?"

CHAPTER SEVEN

With the most energy she had shown all day, Freya jumped to her feet, and the rest of the kids quickly joined her. Jarrett glanced at his watch, happy to see it still worked but shocked by the time. The Race to Erase had started more than thirty minutes ago, so they were already behind.

If, that is, they had actually wanted to enter the race.

"Which we don't!" Jarrett said, completing his thought out loud. "We don't want to be in the race."

"Obviously," Lina agreed. "But to get you out of here, we want people to believe you are. So you have to at least be heading in the right direction. We need to get you on track."

"How are we supposed to get on track?" Jarrett asked.

"The finish line is in New Mexico, and that's thousands of miles away! You know how many guzzlers we'd need to get there?"

"No big deal," Lina said. "I have my own FF."

"You're eleven today, like us, right?" Agnes asked. "Flying around your property in a FuelFlighter is one thing. But we're way too young for an FF pilot's license out in public."

Now it was Lina's turn to roll her eyes. "Oh, please. Don't you remember when I said I get whatever I want?"

With that, Lina herded them inside the mansion and onto a glass elevator. They shot up to the sixth floor, where the elevator door slid open at what Jarret figured was Lina's room. After seeing the rest of the mansion, it was a lot smaller than he expected. Shaped like a perfect circle about the size of half a basketball court, the room was decorated like a cozy hangout.

Sharing a look of surprise with Agnes, Jarrett took in the room as they all stepped off the elevator and the door slid shut behind them. Comfy-looking couches lined the walls under the large bay windows. Thick yellow shag carpeting covered the floor. There was even a brick pizza oven that glowed warmly with a crackling fire. The room didn't have the same energy as the Lina he knew. He figured her room would be all smooth and sleek. Maybe he didn't really know her that well after all.

The air smelled like it'd been sprayed with popcorn-scented air freshener, and the carpet and furniture looked brand-new. Something about it all made Jarrett feel a little sorry for Lina. Had she set up this perfect room to have friends over? And were they the first kids to actually visit?

Only the high table in the center of the room seemed out of place. It had a control panel on it, and Lina hurried straight to it. Agnes, on the other hand, wasted no time plopping down on one of the plush couches and putting up her feet.

"Whoa, that's nice to sit. I need a breather," she said, sinking into the deep cushions. "Hey, Lina, who decorated your bedroom?"

With her hands moving over the control panel, Lina shrugged. "I did, naturally. I'll show it to you guys sometime."

"Um, Lina," Agnes said. "We're seeing it right now."

"Oh, ha," Lina said. "This isn't my bedroom, goofball. This is my FuelFlighter."

With a grin, Lina slammed her hand down on the control panel. There was a tiny tremor, and then the FF lifted gently into the air, turned gracefully, and began gliding through the lower atmosphere. *Whoa!* Jarrett, Malik, and Freya went to the windows to check out the view.

Jarrett was impressed by the surprise takeoff. And he had to give it to Lina, she was a good pilot. "Nice one, Lina."

She smiled. "On the pink FF, I couldn't show off because of the autopilot. But flying is what I love to do. I call my ship *Effugere Tellurem*. That means—"

"That means 'escape Earth,'" Freya said as she gazed out the window.

Lina did a double take and then nodded. "How'd you know that?"

"My grandparents made me learn Latin," Freya answered. "They taught me every language but kidspeak."

"Huh," Lina said, already sounding a little bored. "Anyway, I'm taking us out west toward New Mexico. We won't go all the way, just in the right direction."

As the landscape whizzed beneath them, Jarrett watched it change from forest, to city, to abandoned farms, to dusty landscapes, then back to forest again. For a second, Jarrett worried that they'd been flying in a circle, but then he could see the trees below them were taller and older than the trees surrounding Lina's mansion.

"Does that pizza oven work?" Agnes called from the couch, and when Malik gave her a look that said he was surprised she was hungry, she said, "What? I eat when I get nervous."

This was news to Jarrett. "You never get nervous, Aggie."

"Can you blame me after today?" she responded, and no, he couldn't.

"It's a holo-flame oven," Lina told her. "If you want a pizza, just talk to it."

Agnes hopped up to order a pizza. Jarrett turned to Malik, who was standing quietly on his own. This was Jarrett's chance. "Hey," he said.

Malik shrugged in response and kept looking out the window. He'd been acting strangely since they woke up out on the lawn. Probably just worried about the robots. Jarrett wanted to say something to take his mind off their worries.

"I bet you're excited about the idea of entering the Race to Erase, right?" Jarrett said. "Even though we're just pretending . . ."

After a second, Malik asked, "What do you mean?"

"The race is about catching stuff, and . . ." Jarrett left the last part hanging.

Malik shrugged again and still didn't look. ". . . and I like catching stuff."

"So do Slicer and Dicer," Freya said ominously. She was sitting on the floor, her huge boots out in front of her.

"Okay, okay!" pleaded Agnes. "We get it! We're being pursued by asteroid killers. Can we bring down the level of sheer terror, please?"

As if to answer her, a gentle *zing, zap* alarm sounded, indicating an incoming hologram.

Lina went pale. "That's my brother's bell. Tommy's coming. Hide."

"Hide?" Agnes spluttered. Now she sounded like she was at the end of her rope. "Where?"

"Just do it!" Lina insisted. "He might have figured out you have the spheres!"

The kids did their best. Jarrett and Malik slipped behind a curtain, Agnes tossed her pizza on a table and jumped behind a chair, and Freya slid under the table just as Tommy's hologram popped into the air next to Lina and started looking around. "What are you doing, Lina?"

"Hi, Tommy." Her voice sounded easy, casual. "I just gave my . . . friends? . . . a ride home."

"Then why are you two states away and heading in the wrong direction? I know you're desperate for friends, Lina, but do you really have to go that far to find them?" he said.

Ugh, Jarret thought from behind the curtain. *Tommy is the worst!*

"No, don't answer," Tommy was saying to Lina. "That will take too long, and I don't care. Just get back here. We need to find those spheres, and find them now."

"Spheres?" Lina tried to sound confused but wasn't that good of an actress.

"Yes, spheres, Lina," Tommy said. "I figured out why I

can't track them right now. The Ponies have gone dark for some reason."

"Huh," Lina said. "Did you tell Mom and Dad that they're missing?"

Tommy waved that idea away. "No, Lina, I didn't. I'll take care of it. But I have to work fast."

"What's the big rush?" Lina asked. "Besides them being worth a trillion dollars?"

With a sigh that said the answer should be obvious, Tommy explained, "To keep the Ponies top secret, I programmed the computers to wipe out all records of them tonight, right after the end of the Race to Erase. After that, I won't be able to track them at all, even if they're turned on."

"Oh, that's . . . interesting . . . ," Lina said.

More annoyed than ever, Tommy snapped, "Just get back here and help find them now, okay?"

He didn't wait for an answer. Tommy blipped out.

"Well, see you later," Lina said. At first Jarrett thought she was talking to Tommy. But as they all emerged from hiding, Lina was piloting the FF down to a small clearing in the woods. She landed the ship smoothly and flicked the switch that opened the hatch. Lina drummed her fingers on the control panel. When the others only stared at her, she told them, "Like I said, see you later. Scoot."

Agnes blinked. "Did you just *scoot* us?"

Glancing out the door, Jarrett could see only scary trees and weird rocks. "You can't just leave us out here, Lina. Our phones are busted! We have no way to call for help!"

"I don't have a choice. You'll be fine?" Her reassurance came out like a question. Even she couldn't hide the doubt in her voice. "I could always kind of shake you out of the FF like I did last time."

The others protested, and Lina rolled her eyes. "Oh, grow up. Just stay here. No one will look for you. You'll be fine as long as those Ponies, *which you stole,* are dark. You're the four heroes from the Climate Club, right? You know how to fight nature. You'll be fine. I'll figure out how to get those spheres out of your hands and come back to this exact spot to get you. In the meantime, show nature who's boss! *Scoot!*"

They did just that, reluctantly but quickly. Once they were all outside, the hatch slid shut without another word from Lina and the round FF lifted into the air, a smoky trail of exhaust in its wake. With Lina gone, the four kids stood around for a few seconds, unsure of what to do next, and then Freya took a seat next to a giant tree.

"Careful!" Jarrett warned her, eyeing the network of thick roots that had snaked above the ground and intertwined around the base of the tree.

"It's okay," Freya assured him. "My grandparents love

trees. Mostly, I like them because they're good for putting in songs. They rhyme with so many different words, like *bees, knees, fleas—*"

"Let's do a mash-up game," Malik interrupted. They all looked at him as if to say this was the last thing they wanted to do. "I mean, it's something to do while we wait for Lina to come back. Let's combine ballroom dancing and tightrope walking."

Agnes was the only one to take Malik up on the challenge. Walking along one of the roots like an acrobat on a high wire, she asked, "How old do you think this tree is? Like, a year?"

"No way, too big." Malik joined Agnes on one of the roots, trying to balance as he performed two small leaps. Then, out of nowhere, added, "My parents are going to be so mad."

With a little spin on one of the roots, Agnes asked, "Why? Because we're being hunted by space robots?"

"Ha, no," Malik said. "I'm not getting to know Lina's parents better. Which means they're probably not going to buy space elevators from my family. That's the only reason I came to that party today."

"The *only* reason?" Agnes asked with a quick look at Jarrett. When Malik didn't respond, Agnes pointed somewhere behind Jarrett. "Oh, look, berries!" she cried, and pulled

Malik toward them. It was clear she was trying to cover up any weirdness between Malik and Jarrett.

"It's not true, you know," Freya said, standing up next to Jarrett.

Confused, Jarrett turned his attention to Freya and asked, "What's not true?"

"This tree might be even younger than a year." Freya put both hands on the trunk of the tree. "I hear they snap right back after just a couple of months. That's why it's okay for companies to do whatever they want. I'll find another young tree to show you."

She stood up, and with a little wave, she walked out of the clearing.

"Freya, come on," Jarrett warned. "It's not a good idea to wander off by yourself!"

Malik chimed in, but his words came out squishy, like his mouth was full. And Agnes responded with something that sounded supportive, but her mouth sounded full too.

"What are you guys eating?" Jarrett demanded.

Malik pointed at a bush behind Jarrett. It was filled with strange-looking berries. "They're good," he said, but it came out like, "Is schmood."

This made Agnes laugh, and purple berry juice dribbled from her mouth.

But Jarrett wasn't laughing. "Spit that out. That could be poisonous!"

"Is schmood!" Agnes insisted. Which made her laugh even harder.

Jarrett shook his head. "Why can't you just leave stuff alone? Nature isn't a restaurant, where everything is all safe. We need to keep it together."

Ignoring him, Malik said, "Let's mash up a spinning top and the balance beam, Agnes. See who can spin the longest on these roots."

"Shookay," she told Malik. After a huge swallow and a swipe across her mouth with the back of her hand, Agnes said, "Come on, Jar. You're overreacting. This is the woods!" She did a little spin, like someone on a commercial showing off how amazing their perfume smelled, all the while staying balanced on the thick root. "People go on vacation in the woods because it's so relaxing. Or they used to in old movies, anyway." Still spinning around with her arms out, she continued, "There's nothing in here that's bad—"

Then she was gone.

What? Jarrett's mind lurched. Agnes had dropped out of sight.

Moving at exactly the same time, Jarrett and Malik jerked toward her to help.

"Ouch!" Malik cried. His foot had slipped in between two roots up to his shin, and now he was stuck.

But Jarrett kept moving. Scrambling over the roots without thinking, he leapt to where Agnes had disappeared. He saw her hands first, clutching two rocks at the edge of a hole just a few feet from the roots of the tree, and his eyes followed her arms down into a pit that reminded him of a mouth that wanted to swallow her now-dangling body whole.

But, of course, Agnes was laughing.

"What is wrong with you?" he asked. "How is this funny?"

"Such a worrywart, Jar," she said. "These rocks are perfect handles, see? Just where they should be in case somebody trips. And besides, how deep can this pit be anyway?"

Jarrett didn't want to think about that. He couldn't see the bottom from where he stood at the top.

"Um, guys, a little help . . . ?" It was Malik. He was still stuck.

"Here." Jarrett crouched next to Agnes. "Take my hand, and I'll pull you out."

"Thanks," Malik said.

"He's talking to me!" Agnes shouted. She grabbed on to Jarrett's wrist as he clasped hers, and as he started to pull her up, Agnes let go of the other rock. Now her body was dangling, her legs and one arm flailing. Jarrett dropped to his knees to keep from toppling into the pit but managed to hold on to her. His knee loosened a rock, and it tumbled over the edge. It came within inches of hitting Agnes in the head and disappeared into the darkness.

He didn't hear it hit the bottom of the pit. *If there is a bottom*, Jarrett thought.

Luckily, Freya had come back to the clearing, and she braced herself just behind Jarrett. She pulled back on his shoulders. But it still wasn't enough in the loose dirt. Now both Freya and Jarrett were sliding toward the edge. In seconds, all three of them would fall.

They needed a better plan, Jarrett knew. "Grab the rocks again, Agnes."

When she had regripped them, he stood up and glanced around desperately.

"Ha, I don't know how long I can hold on." Agnes was still joking, but a little worry had entered her tone. "I hope there's a soft landing below."

There! Jarrett sprinted about ten feet opposite them, where two small saplings were struggling to grow in the shade of the giant tree.

"Where are you going?" Freya asked.

"Just here," Jarrett said. "I'll grab this baby tree. Freya, you take my other hand. We'll make a chain and we'll pull her out."

The sphere in his hand felt strange rubbing against the

tree. Freya's hand was cool in his other. She reached down toward Agnes. But their fingers were too far apart. The sapling was snapping in two from Jarrett's weight, and he could see that Agnes's fingers were slipping off the rocks—

"We need . . . more . . . people," Jarrett said through gritted teeth. "Malik!"

Just then Malik yanked his foot free from the roots, leaving his sneaker behind. He took Freya's hand and leaned toward Agnes.

We still need one more person, thought Jarrett. *We need a fifth person to help us.*

But then the tree bent more, and Malik's hand finally touched Agnes's. The four were a long human chain now, and when their hands were all connected—

A blinding, bright flash exploded.

We need, Jarrett was still thinking. *We need—*

QUICK! TURN TO PAGE 185!

CHAPTER NINE

*Y*ou.

Jarrett, Freya, and Malik were in midmotion, having just yanked Agnes out of the pit. With a final grunt, Jarrett had pulled as hard as he could on the tree, dragging the rest of them toward him. The energy had flown from him through Freya and Malik—and Agnes had been jerked up and over the lip of the hole.

Then their hands had lost their grip on one another as all four fell sprawling onto the ground . . . again.

"Everyone okay?" Malik asked as he rose to retrieve his shoe stuck between the roots.

Offering Freya a hand up, Agnes said a little shakily, "I'm

all right, I guess. I'm just embarrassed about needing rescuing. Thanks, guys."

Jarrett waved that away. "Don't be silly, Aggie. Everyone needs help sometimes." Brushing himself off and getting to his feet, Jarrett blinked. "Did you guys hear any of that while we were touching hands?"

"You mean that weird voice?" Freya said.

"Like four people talking at exactly the same time, right?" Agnes asked.

Jarrett nodded. "They were challenging somebody to fix things. To help us."

"Beyond freaky," Agnes said.

"My hands are not sweaty," Malik said defensively. Agnes and Freya, who had been in the chain on either side of him, both made faces to say, *actually, they kind of are.*

In a tone that indicated she knew it sounded wild, Freya admitted, "I can't remember too much of what the voices said, but I think that was the Four Ponies talking."

"Why?" Jarrett asked. "What makes you think that?"

"Just a gut feeling, I guess. I mean, there were four spheres and there were four voices. Plus, there's this. . . ." Freya held up her hand. The sphere embedded in her palm was no longer dark. It gave off a shockingly bright glow. The sphere had a greenish tint that shone through her skin.

The other three looked at their own palms. With a jolt,

Jarrett saw his sphere glowed with a purplish light. Yellow came from Malik's and red from Agnes's.

"Oh no. Oh no!" Jarrett shoved the hand with the sphere into his pocket, Agnes clasped her hands together, and Malik balled his glowing hand up into a fist as if trying to hide it. The only one who continued to stare at the sphere in her palm was Freya.

Looking a little hypnotized by the light, she sang softly, "Take my hand and we can change the world."

The others shared a worried look. "Freya? You okay?" Agnes asked. When Freya didn't answer, Agnes said, "That's a pretty song. . . . Who's that by?"

"Me, I wrote it, just now," Freya answered, and then she finally brought her eyes up. "Something about us grabbing hands all together must've made the Ponies activate."

"That makes sense," Agnes said, sounding relieved that Freya had snapped out of it.

"Really? Does it?" Jarrett asked doubtfully.

Agnes shrugged. "Well, as much as anything makes sense today."

"It sounded like the voice was talking with someone else," Malik said. "I couldn't hear what that other person was saying, could you?"

The rest of the kids shook their heads.

"Who was that other person?" Agnes asked.

"It was like hearing one side of a phone conversation," Jarrett said. "I could only hear the Ponies talking. Something about making a choice that could change everything?"

"I have no idea who they were they talking to, but I guess if we're the four heroes, that'd make that other person the Fifth Hero," Malik said.

Jarrett wanted to point out that Lina was being sarcastic when she'd called them the four heroes. But why bother? The Fifth Hero sounded like as good a name as any for the mysterious person the Four Ponies were speaking with.

"Let's see if something the Fifth Hero did made a difference," Freya suggested, and they all looked around.

Just the same trees, fallen leaves, weird snaky roots. Everything seemed exactly as it was before to Jarrett. "I don't know. I can't tell. Would the difference be something drastic?"

Turning over a rock, Freya said, "I think the decision is small, but the change would be big?"

Jarrett shrugged. "We have more serious things to worry about," he said. "Tommy said when the spheres are lit up he can track them. He could be on his way right now."

"Good point," Malik said. "I feel like we're walking homing beacons. We need to get out of here."

"We can't leave this spot," Agnes said. "Lina told us not to. She won't be able to find us!"

"But Tommy will find us for sure if we stay," Malik said, and then added, "Worse. Slicer and Dicer will too."

"Okay, fine, we need to move!" Agnes shot back, exasperated. "But where?"

Jarrett held up his finger. *Wait.* The idea was almost fully baked, but still in that fragile phase where even the smallest distraction could derail it. It just needed one more second to finish, and then—*ding!*

"I know a place!"

"Where, Jar?" Agnes asked. "Where should we go?"

"The one place where the only two people who can help us will be," Jarrett said, getting excited. "The finish line of the Race to Erase."

Loud protests erupted from the others and included adjectives like *dumb, dangerous,* and *da-ridiculous.* (Freya shrugged after adding that last adjective. "I like alliteration.")

Holding up his hands for silence, Jarret said, "You guys heard Lina's parents. Dr. and Dr. Limwick said they'd be at the end of the race to hand out the trophy."

"Sure," Agnes said. "I kind of remember that."

Nodding, Jarrett kept going. "The Limwicks are always saving the world from calamities, right? I think they can handle saving the four of us. Like Tommy said, they probably don't even know the spheres are missing. And they'll want to help us. But they also keep super-tight schedules and will probably only stay there for a minute. The race ends at dusk. We need to get there right at dusk!"

Already heading into the woods, Agnes said, "Okay. Let's go. Let's just follow the path to the finish line."

Jarrett pulled her back. "Uh, Aggie? There is no path. This is the wilderness."

"There's always a path!" Agnes cried. She sounded on edge again. "I bet it's like a maze, where we have to solve clues to find our way out."

"No." Jarrett was starting to lose his patience. "This isn't a ride. And it isn't a game. This is real. This is the woods. There is no path. Only scary, bitey things."

As if to prove his point, a giant mosquito buzzed by Jarrett's head with that annoying high-pitched whine. Yuck! Jarrett slapped his ear. He felt the sphere in his palm clunk against his skull, but he thought he might have gotten the tiny bloodsucker.

Then something flashed in front of his face. It looked like a little paper, about the size of a playing card. The card floated in the air before his eyes, and it had a creepy skull on it that looked like it had been drawn with black finger paint.

"What is *that*?" Jarrett asked, and dropped his hand from his ear to reach for the card—but it disappeared with a tiny pop.

"What's what?" Agnes asked.

"You didn't see that?" Jarrett touched his ear again. A card popped in front of his face with an acorn drawn on it. Keeping one hand on his ear, he batted at the card with his other hand. The card spun in the air for a moment before it flew off into the nearby trees.

Suddenly, cards were popping out of thin air all around him. Most showed acorns, but a few were filled with what looked like . . .

"Is that poop?" Jarrett asked.

"Is what poop?" Malik asked.

"Come on, Jar," Agnes said. "Knock it off. I love fun and games as much as the next person, but stop waving your arm around at nothing."

Jarrett kept whacking cards with his free hand, sending them spinning off into the trees. "Do you guys not see this?"

Freya came to stand next to him and peer into the air. "See what?"

"The cards!" Jarrett said. "They have weird paintings on them. Like this one." He pointed at a card. "It's an acorn." He pointed at other cards. "This one is poop, and this is an acorn. It's like texting with a three-year-old."

About fifteen more cards popped up, and they were all poop, poop, poop.

"An *angry* three-year-old," he added.

Three of his sisters were toddler triplets, so Jarrett knew about angry three-year-olds. But this was way out of his league. Jarrett tried shutting his eyes to ignore the images, but when he opened them, there were even more cards. This time they were just an inch or so away from his nose, and they were quivering, as if cross at being ignored. One of an acorn jiggled more than the others.

He could hear the chitter of a squirrel in a nearby bush, and each time it made a sound, the acorn card in front of Jarrett wiggled impatiently.

Jarrett started to understand what was happening. "Oh no."

"Explain, please," Agnes demanded.

More poop and acorn cards popped into the air all around Jarrett. "Oh, nothing. Just my worst nightmare," he said. "I think the animals are talking to me."

"Talking to you?" Freya sounded jealous. "What do you hear?"

"Animal sounds. Like there's a very chatty squirrel over there." Jarrett pointed at the bush.

"We can all hear that squirrel, Jarrett," Malik said.

"But it's not what I'm hearing; it's what I'm seeing."

Agnes still wasn't having it. "Okay, whatever you're doing so we just stay here, it's not going to work. Even if there is no path, we need to get out of here. Sorry, Jar, but that's the way it is."

"Fine, jeez, take it easy, Aggie," Jarrett said. "I guess maybe I'm just tired."

When he dropped his hand from his ear, the cards disappeared. He looked at his hand. It was the one with the Pony in it, and he noticed its violet light didn't seem as bright. "Hey—" he started to say, wanting to tell the others.

"We're going," Agnes said. "We're going before the robots get here."

She was marching off when Freya said, "Hold on. You're going the wrong way."

"How do you know?" Malik asked.

When Freya pointed up into the sky, Agnes sighed in frustration. "Oh no, not you too. Are you seeing ghosts or something?"

"The sun. It rhymes with *everything*!" Freya explained. "And my grandparents showed me how to use it."

"How can you use the sun?" Jarrett asked.

"Oh, right," Malik said. "The sun! We can tell which direction we're going. We need to go west, right, toward New Mexico?"

"Come on," Freya said. Once again, Jarrett was surprised by her sudden leadership. Following Freya, the group pushed through the low underbrush that had managed to sprout up out of the dry ground. A branch tore at Jarrett's shirt, ripping off fabric at the shoulder. The outfit was already ruined, so not the end of the world, but Jarrett had the feeling the tree wanted his flesh, not his shirt.

Finally, after ten minutes of stumbling around, which seemed more like an hour to Jarrett, they emerged from the forest and found themselves on the narrow bank of a raging river. White foam created by rapids rushed just inches below them in a blur. Bits of brightly colored plastic and other garbage intermingled with dead fish had been pushed up onto the shore by the force of the water. How were they going to cross this?

"Careful not to fall in!" Jarrett warned the others.

But he wondered if anyone could hear him over the thundering river. Just a few hundred feet away, the river disappeared into a cloud of mist and boulders. Jarrett had never seen anything like it.

"How can the water just end?" he wondered out loud.

"That's not the end of the river," Malik answered, yelling to be heard over the roar of the water. "That's where it turns into a waterfall."

Waterfall? Jarrett stopped walking so he could look more closely. Of course. The river didn't end—if anything, that seemed like the starting line for it to really get going.

Through the heavy mist, he could see a series of boulders standing guard. But now he could tell from the way the water splashed and swirled around the boulders that the river continued past them with deafening force as it shot over a cliff.

The waterfall made the idea of falling into the river even more terrifying. Whoever did would be swept along by the current and straight over that cliff. Why would anyone ever want to go on a canoe or whatever people did on water for "fun"?

Jarrett looked more closely. Once again, he couldn't believe he had missed something so important. Those weren't boulders. At least, not all of them. There were guzzlers caught against the rocks. And something else.

"Those are people!" he cried.

CHAPTER TEN

No one heard Jarrett call out over the waterfall's roar. Up ahead, the other kids had continued picking their way away along the rocky path. It abruptly ended at a rock wall that blocked the path and jutted out into the river. To keep moving ahead they'd either have to walk into the river to get around the rock or head back into the woods. Freya, Malik, and Agnes were taking turns leaning out around the rock wall, checking out something up the river.

His heart pounding, Jarrett glanced back out at the small group of people who seemed impossibly balanced on top of the waterfall. Half of their bodies were submerged in the water as they clung to the largest of the boulders at the top of the cliff.

"Guys," Jarrett called to his friends. No response. He took a deep breath and shouted, "Guys!"

This got Agnes's attention. Finally. She tapped Freya's and Malik's shoulders in front of her, and they worked their way back to Jarrett.

"There's a crashed FF up there!" Agnes told him, shouting to be heard. "Just around that rock wall. You can't see it from here!"

"Great," Jarrett said, and pointed in the other direction to the waterfall. "But those are people!"

Following his gesture, her eyes widened. "Oh no," she gasped. "There's one . . . two . . . three . . . four of them."

"Two kids and their parents, looks like," Malik said. "What are they doing?"

"Trying to stay alive!" Freya answered. Her normally calm face had gone red, as if she wasn't used to so much shouting.

Jarrett tried to piece everything together. He imagined the family's guzzlers running out of gas just as they were zipping along the river . . . or maybe they'd been trying to cross it at a shallow spot. Either way, they'd tumbled into the water and been swept downriver by the current, until the guzzlers had caught between two boulders, creating a temporary safety net between them and the edge of the waterfall. But the water was building up, and soon it would burst through.

"We have to do something!" Jarrett grabbed for his phone

before he remembered it was dead. He felt helpless. He'd never realized how much he relied on it. But then again, even if they could call for help, Jarrett didn't think it would arrive in time.

Malik rushed up and down the line of trees. "Maybe if we can find a log, we can push it toward them . . . like this!" He pulled a dead stick out from the underbrush.

Freya shook her head. "Won't that just knock into them and shove them over the waterfall?"

"You might be right," Malik said. "But we need to let them know we're here."

Jumping up and down, Jarrett waved his arms and shouted, "Hey! Hey! Over here!"

"No! Stop!" Agnes dropped to her knees and pulled the rest of them down, too, so the family couldn't see them over the low scrub brush along the edge of the river. "What if this is all one big fake-out?"

"Does it look like that family is faking?" Malik asked.

"No, really, listen," Agnes insisted. "This could be a trap set up by Tommy to capture us."

"I don't know Tommy, but I don't think that's really his style, do you, Aggie?" Jarrett countered. "He'd just swoop in and grab us. He's sending Slicer and Dicer the killer robots, not an accident-prone family of four."

"All right, they're probably not secret ninjas," Agnes

admitted. "But still, we can't take a chance that their phones or guzzlers don't automatically scan our faces. Tommy has probably hacked into every computer on the planet, and he'd be able to find us in a second."

Okay, maybe she had a point about that. Jarrett unstrapped his backpack and shoved a hand inside. He dug quickly around party streamers, a HAPPY BIRTHDAY banner, and the noisemakers he'd smashed when he'd flown off the guzzler. He'd been too embarrassed to pull out the decorations before. Now he jammed his hand underneath them and the remaining bits of packing popcorn and grabbed four of the five masks he'd tucked inside there this morning.

"Um, let's see, I've got the classic laughing with tears emoji, the flexing arm one, the light bulb, or the hot dog emoji," Jarrett said.

With hands up, Malik was shaking his head. "No way. I'm not wearing a hot dog on my face. I don't care how much danger we're in."

"He's got a point, Jar," Agnes said. "Why do you even have these? Nobody uses emojis anymore."

"They were on sale super cheap and, you know, for Lina's birthday party. I thought they were funny. But they seemed so silly after we got a look at her mansion. There's a fifth one in here, for Lina."

Agnes said, "Or the Fifth Hero."

She was kind of joking, Jarrett knew, but he imagined the word *you* echoing in the air again.

Having taken the mask with the flexing arm, Freya peered inside at its lining and said, "Let's just turn them inside out. They're plain on the inside."

"Good plan," Jarrett said.

All four turned the masks inside out and slid them over their heads. Each one was a slightly different shade of yellow, the kind of mask that squashed your nose but wasn't too tight. Jarrett could still make out everyone's eyebrows and lips. The material had that new-costume smell—a strong chemical scent, but it would wear off after a minute or two. The best part was that the material was so sheer it didn't really affect vision; it was just like wearing sunglasses.

"Okay, I can work with this," Malik said.

"Seriously?" Agnes said. "I feel ridiculous."

"Same here, Aggie," Jarrett said. "But it will block any facial recognition software that might be running in the area."

"Good enough for me," Malik said. He reached down to the river but yanked back his hand the instant it connected with the water. "Ouch," he said, as if he'd gotten burned.

Worried, Jarrett asked, "What happened?"

"I felt a shock," Malik said, gazing at his hand. "Not too painful, just weird."

More cautiously, Malik touched the water again. This

time his hand left an imprint on the surface like he'd just put it into wet cement.

"Whoa, what's wrong with this river?" he said.

Slightly dazed, Malik pinched his fingers together and pulled his hand up a few feet over the surface. A glittering string of liquid, like clear taffy, led from his hand down into the river. He stretched the string a little more and then let go. It snapped back into the water with a little splash and managed to keep its string shape for a few seconds before disappearing into the current.

"What is happening?" Malik said. "The water is like glue or clay. . . ."

The others stuck their hands in the water and splashed them around. Nothing special happened—it was just regular water. But Malik continued pulling up strings of liquid and was actually able to wrap two strands around each other. Tiny bits of trash shone through the water, and it made Jarrett think of pollution and the climate and . . . the Ponies.

"Didn't Tommy and his parents say one of the Ponies would react with water?" Jarrett asked.

"That's true," Freya said.

"Try your other hand, Malik," Agnes suggested. "The one without the Pony."

Malik released the braid of water, and it plopped back into the river. He stuck his other hand in the water and moved it around, but now the river just flowed through his fingers. "What is going on?"

"Let's worry about that later," Jarrett said. "Right now, can you, I don't know, shape the water into something to help that family?"

"Like what?" Malik asked.

"I don't know," Jarrett said. "You like seahorses, right? Maybe a horse?"

With an "it's worth a try" shrug, Malik scooped his hand with the Pony back into the water. It was like watching someone trying to make a snowman in an avalanche with one hand. After a few seconds, Malik had molded the water into the shape of a horselike creature that a preschooler might make out of clay. With a shove of his hand, Malik sent the horse across the water and over toward the family.

The son, who was maybe seven, stared at the horse with wide eyes. His gaze traveled to the shore. The four masked kids waved at him frantically. Jarrett could only imagine what they looked like with their kind of creepy yellow masks on.

"Hop on!" Malik yelled while gesturing what he meant by pretending to mount a horse and hold its reins. "He'll bring you to safety!"

The rest of the kid's family still hadn't noticed them on the shore. Nervously, the kid climbed over the dam made by the guzzlers, and then climbed on top of the horse and—

Fell right through.

Of course he did, Jarrett thought. That horsey thing was made of water! What did they expect?

"Oops," Malik said. "I'll need to work on that."

"You think?" Agnes said.

The little boy was swept against the blockade of guzzlers. Finally, the girl noticed, and they could hear her shout in panic. She grabbed the boy by the leg and pulled him back to the relative safety of the rocks and the parents' waiting arms.

But the boy slamming into the wall of guzzlers had dislodged one of them. And after two or three seconds of withstanding the violent torrent of the river, it went tumbling over the top of the waterfall. Now there were only three guzzlers between the family and a very quick, but possibly painful, ending.

By this point, the parents had turned their attention to the shore and spotted the kids.

"Hi! We just made things worse!" Jarrett said, waving, grinning like an idiot. "We'll save you if we don't kill you first! For four heroes we're sure doing a lousy job!"

"I have an idea," Malik said, and spun the water with one finger.

His finger created a whirlpool, and then Malik pushed his hand—the one with the Pony—all the way into the water as he kept swirling. Almost instantly the whirlpool expanded and got deeper. Soon it was as wide as the circle he could make with this arm, and it went down to the riverbed. He pushed the whirlpool out toward the family, and it kept expanding as it went.

"Nice shot!" Agnes said.

When it reached the dam made of guzzlers, it stalled a little and then started pulling the guzzlers loose. They wobbled in the current and went over the side of the waterfall. After bouncing off the guzzlers, the whirlpool started heading back toward the kids.

Now the whirlpool was the only thing blocking the raging river from washing the family over the cliff. And it was moving away from them. Soon they would be totally unprotected.

Jarrett couldn't believe it. "You're making things worse, Malik. They're going to get swept over!"

CHAPTER ELEVEN

With all the splashing and yelling confusion, Malik somehow managed to stay calm.

He shouted to the family, "Walk in the whirlpool, you guys!"

They gaped at him for a second. Then, with no other choice, the family let go of the boulders and stepped into the whirlpool. Their feet touched the rocky river bottom, but for now the shape of the whirlpool was holding. The family was able to walk on the riverbed as the whirlpool moved back toward Malik on the shore.

"No way," Jarrett said to Agnes.

"I know, it's amazing, right?" she agreed.

"No, it's not that." Jarrett shook his head. "Malik gets to

make water horses and whirlpools, and I get the language of poop."

Agnes laughed and then clapped a hand over her mouth. "Sorry, Jar Jar. At least you know what your Pony's power is, unlike me."

The whirlpool was falling apart. It was no longer touching the riverbed, and the family's feet were getting wet in about five inches of water. It looked like there might just be a few seconds left before it completely disintegrated. As the Climate Club reached to help the family out of the water, the boy darted out of the river and sprinted past all of them.

Freya tried to stop him, but she wasn't fast enough, and the boy plunged into the woods.

Jarrett couldn't really blame him. He was sure they looked kind of weird in their masks.

"No, Sydney!" the mom shouted, and the dad called, "Come back, Sydney!"

Trying to lunge for his son, the dad fell back into the water, and the mom and girl turned to help him, just as the whirlpool finally gave out. The current knocked the family over. Freya, Malik, and Agnes reached down to offer their hands.

"Don't worry, I'll get him!" Jarrett said. Without thinking, he ran into the woods after the boy. Jarrett caught up to him in a few seconds at the intersection of two trails. The kid was standing there, unmoving.

Jarrett reached for the boy's shoulder. "Sydney—?"

The kid started shouting at the top of his lungs. "Help! Help! Help!"

At first, Jarrett wasn't too surprised, figuring this was Sydney's response to nature. Wasn't this reaction exactly the reason the Calamity Corporation always warned people not to go into the woods?

But when Sydney kept shouting, Jarrett got more concerned. And that concern turned to fear when, in between Sydney's shouts, he heard a low huffing sound. He swiveled his head to see what was making it. *Oh no.*

A bear. A giant, hulking brown bear, at least two hundred pounds. No, not just one bear. On the other side of Sydney, on the second path, there was a second, smaller bear. This bear looked to be maybe fifty pounds.

They must be standing right between a momma bear and her cub.

Were you supposed to run or stand still when you saw a bear? Were you supposed to be quiet or make noise? Jarrett had no clue, and he'd never wanted to ask his broken phone questions more than he did right this second.

It was hard to think straight with the two bears staring at

them and with Sydney shouting. Jarrett put his finger to his own mouth to show Sydney that he had to be quiet. Jarrett started to say "Shhh," when something completely new happened.

Cards, like the ones he had seen earlier in the clearing, popped up out of his mouth. These had pictures that looked even less sophisticated than the finger-painted ones from before.

Poop. Poop. Acorn. Poop.

The cards hung in the air for a split second, then disappeared with bright flashes combined with growling sounds. The forest around them went silent. It was a silence that could only be described as confused. And Sydney was staring at him with the same confusion.

"Did you just say, 'Poop, poop, acorn, poop?'" he asked.

Jarrett wouldn't have believed it would be possible to blush in this situation, but he did. He'd just have to try again. When he tried to speak a second time through his hand, there was more poop and more acorns. It seemed that his vocabulary was that of a squirrel. He needed to broaden his word choice. Maybe he could just say what he wanted to the momma bear?

"We're not going to hurt you," he said out loud through his hand. Cards flew out of his mouth and spun into the air, each popping into a growling or mewling sound. Instead of calming her down, the words just made the bear more furious. The momma bear began rocking back and forth and dragging her five-inch claws into the dirt.

Jarrett pulled Sydney a little closer to him, not sure what was about to happen—

"What!"

The shocked cry came from Freya. She had burst into the clearing and gotten a good look at the situation. She put her hand to her mouth and sucked in air in a panic.

Tiny electric sparks flew from her hand, and the branches on nearby trees bent toward her. A few leaves even tore free and smacked her in the face.

Then Freya let out the breath through her hand, and—

WHOOSH!

Like a cartoon character being yanked off the screen by a giant hook, Freya was lifted off her feet and blown backward out of the clearing toward the river.

There was a moment where everyone—both bears and humans—were too stunned to move. Had that really just happened?

Then Jarrett was in motion, taking advantage of the distraction Freya had accidentally created. Grabbing Sydney by the arm, he sprinted for a nearby tree and scrambled up. The bear must have thought he was trying to get into position to attack her cub. She lunged for him with her front paws, barely missing.

The two boys huddled in a fork of the tree made by a branch and the trunk. Furious, the bear lumbered over to the tree and began clawing at the bark, while pushing the whole tree back and forth. She was going to shake the kids out of the tree if it was the last thing she did.

From this angle, Jarrett got a close-up look at the bear. Her eyes were milky, and gray goo oozed from them, dripping onto her facial fur like tears. Her black coat draped on her pointy shoulders the way a blanket would on a clothesline. And her breath was awful. He could almost smell how sick she was.

He thought about the dead fish and the trash along the banks of the river. The bear must be starving, trying to feed herself and her cub, who was now huddled close to its mom. The humans might be able to find a way to escape Earth, but what about all the animals? Jarrett could barely believe it, but he started to feel sorry for them.

Still, the bear's sharp claws certainly seemed healthy enough as they sank into the bark of the tree, leaving long, deep scratches. Maybe the animals weren't so helpless after all.

"Whoa!" Sydney shouted. But his tone was different. He

sounded more amazed than scared. When Jarrett looked over at Sydney, the boy was pointing up at the sky.

Jarrett glanced up.

Two flaming streaks were shooting across the sky. Were those meteors? Heat and fire created a blur around the objects. And they were headed straight to the kids.

The mother bear was so focused on tearing down the tree, it took mewling from her cub to turn her attention to the sky. Nose sniffing at the air, she turned and looked up beyond Jarrett and Sydney. Jarrett could see the two fireballs reflected in her cloudy eyes.

The two bears turned and ran, heading into the woods and away from the river.

Sydney held up his phone to take a video of the meteor things, and the moment he did, the streaks reversed course, almost like a housefly bouncing off a window. Whatever they were, they didn't want to be videoed.

The fireballs made such a sharp turnaround that they lost their speed and plummeted to Earth, a couple miles away. Even from that distance, the impact created two explosions, both equally deafening.

"What . . . ?" Freya said. She'd run back into the clearing and was still out of breath. "What were those things?"

Jarrett knew exactly what they were. "Slicer and Dicer have landed."

CHAPTER TWELVE

Earning themselves a few more scratches from hungry branches, Freya and Jarrett led Sydney back to the riverbank, where his parents pulled him into their arms and his sister joined the group hug.

"Freya . . . ," Jarrett said as they watched the family embrace. "Do you want to talk about . . . ?" He looked pointedly at her hand, but she just shook her head, very clearly saying, *I'm not ready to talk about the fact that I can create wind.*

When the family finally separated, Sydney peered up at Jarrett. "Why are you wearing masks? Why do your hands glow?"

Jarrett looked at his hand and Freya's. Their lights were dimmer than before. Malik's palm was completely dark, as if an internal battery had run dry. The only one at full power still was Agnes.

To Sydney he said, "Long story, buddy." And to his friends, "We have to go. Slicer and Dicer are here."

Malik nodded, and Freya looked grim. But before they could say goodbye, Sydney asked, "Are you superheroes?"

Ruffling Sydney's hair, his mom chuckled. "He's really into that action show *Jessie and the Flying Fabubots.*"

"Um, no," Agnes said. "Well, maybe heroes, according to our sarcastic friend Lina. But I don't know about the super part."

"If you're not superheroes, why did you help us?" Sydney's sister asked. "Don't you want to win?"

"Win what?" Jarrett asked.

"Aren't you in the Race to Erase, like us?" Sydney asked. "We haven't caught any bats yet, have you? Did you know they're almost extinct and super hard to find? Don't you want to get off Earth before it's too late?"

The race! Jarrett couldn't believe this kid still had the race on his mind after almost getting killed. Twice. "You think winning the race is so important that we'd leave you dangling over a waterfall?" he asked.

Sydney seemed to think that over for a second and then shrugged. "I don't know. But I do know I wasn't even going to be out here today."

His father picked Sydney up and hugged him again. "Sydney's got bad asthma and can't usually get outside because of the pollution. But for some reason, today has been better."

"Still," said his mom. "I think we'll leave the race to others. We've had enough excitement for one day."

Well, their good day might be about to change if we stick around, Jarrett thought. If they didn't leave the family now, they'd *all* be in danger from Slicer and Dicer.

Jarrett and the others tried to bid the family goodbye, but Sydney stopped them. "Wait!"

Jarrett took a breath, trying to be patient with the little kid, but he could feel the seconds ticking by. He wanted to shout, "Don't you get it, kid? Space robots are coming!" Instead, he asked, "What's up, Sydney?"

"I saw something from my guzzler when we came in," Sydney said. "That's why we crashed, you know. We tried guzzling on the water and—"

"Sydney, buddy, we've got to go," Malik interrupted. He looked as impatient as Jarrett felt.

But Sydney wouldn't be stopped. "It's like a pit or something," he said, "and you'll get trapped."

"Oh, he's right!" Sydney's sister pointed up along the path, where it ended at the outcropping. "I saw it too. If you go that way into the woods, you'll probably fall into an old quarry that's filled with water."

"It looked so deep," Sydney added. "You won't be able to get out."

That wouldn't be good, Jarrett thought. They'd be sitting ducks for Slicer and Dicer. "Wow, lucky for us you were able to get outside today!" he told Sydney.

And what if he hadn't been out here? What if the air quality had kept him inside and Sydney hadn't given them that warning? For some reason, Jarrett thought of the choice that the Fifth Hero had made.

"Once my phone dries out, there should be enough battery power to call for help," the dad said. "We'll be okay. Good luck with the Race to Erase, and thanks for saving us!"

With goodbye waves and Malik leading the way, the heroes left the family and headed back up the path.

Where the path ended, they had a choice: they could push their way through the thick branches back into the woods, or they could walk out into the river for just a few steps to get around the rock wall. After hearing about the quarry trap in the forest, the choice was a pretty easy one to make. As they waded into the water and came around the other side of the wall, a new path opened up. Jarrett could see what the others had seen before.

A four-person FF had crashed into the bank of the river, digging into the soft ground and knocking over a couple of trees. Whoever had been flying must have escaped through the hatch and left it open.

As they approached, Agnes pulled off her mask. "Whew. That's better. That thing is hot."

Jarrett gave Agnes an alarmed look. "What?" she asked. "It's okay. The robots are after these. . . ." She raised her hand with the Pony. "Not these . . ." And waved that hand around her face.

She was right. If there was no one around, they might as well be able to breathe more easily. The rest of them pulled their masks up over their heads. "Just be ready to put them back on," Jarrett warned.

Malik poked his face through the hatch of the ship. "Hello?" When no one responded, he signaled everyone to follow him inside.

The ship was empty and dark, except for the small amount of light streaming through the windows. This FuelFlighter was the opposite of Lina's. Compared to her aircraft, this was a flying shed. The walls in here were exposed metal, like no one had ever bothered to cover them up.

Jarrett flicked a light switch near the door, and Malik went behind the control panel to try to start the engine. But nothing lit up. "Maybe the hatch needs to be closed for it to power on?"

"Worth a try," Jarrett said. "Help me, Freya."

Freya gripped the top of the hatch and Jarrett crouched to grab the bottom; together they were able to swing the hatch back in toward the ship. They groaned with the strain, but it finally swung shut with a dull click.

"Try the controls now," Agnes said.

Malik did, but the console remained dark. Then the FF began to vibrate. **BOOM. BOOM.** The others looked hopefully at Malik.

"I'm not making that sound," he said.

"I can guess who is," Agnes said.

So could Jarrett.

BOOM. BOOM. The vibrations continued; something was approaching. *Actually,* Jarret thought, *it's two somethings. Slicer and Dicer.*

The Climate Club had to get out of the ship. Now.

Jarrett and Freya went to open the hatch again, but this time it wouldn't budge.

"The hatch is stuck!" Jarrett shouted, his voice rising to new levels of panic.

That click sound must have been the lock sliding into place. They were sitting ducks inside the FF.

Jarrett looked at his palm. Even if he wanted to, there weren't any animals for him to talk to here in the ship. And what good would any animal do against satellite-destroying robots?

"I can't touch the water from in here," Malik said, following Jarrett's train of thought.

"And I don't know what my sphere can do, if anything," Agnes said. "Freya?"

Freya looked at her palm. She still seemed freaked out, and Jarrett hated to push her, but they needed to get out of this trap before the robots arrived.

"Freya, when you created that wind, there were little sparks, right?" Jarrett said.

"Hold on, you can make wind?" Agnes said, sounding a little jealous.

Freya nodded and smiled at Agnes, then answered Jarrett's question. "Like baby lightning," she said. "Yeah, I saw that too."

To check, she held her hand in front of her with the sphere in her palm facing herself—

"No!" Jarrett swatted her hand away from her face just as a bolt of electricity shot out of her palm. It fired past her head and burned a small hole in the thick wall of the drone . . . near where Malik was standing.

"Watch where you point that thing!" Malik said.

"Don't worry," Freya said, clearly shaken. "I won't do that again."

BOOM. BOOM.

The FF's window was facing toward the forest, so they couldn't see them, but Slicer and Dicer were getting closer.

"Well, we need to do something," Agnes said, waving her hand with the Pony in the air like she could save them if she just made the right kind of jazz hands.

"Maybe I can blow the robots back?" Freya said. She bent down, made a tube with her fingers, and blew through the hole she'd burned through the wall.

The hole was on the other side of the ship from where Slicer and Dicer were approaching, so Jarrett wasn't sure what good it would do. But then the FF shuddered. It rose in the air, one side still stuck in the ground, and then settled back.

"Blow harder!" Jarrett shouted.

Freya took a deep breath and blew out—hard—creating a mini tornado. The FF jerked up out of the ground about twenty feet into the air and spun around like a top.

"Freya!" Agnes shouted. "Stop!"

"If I stop, we'll drop to the ground," Freya called back. "I'll try to move us toward the west."

Freya blew even harder through the hole. Now the FF spun like an amusement park ride, the one that pushes riders up against the walls as it spins and the floor drops out. The four kids were like points on a compass stuck up against different sections of the wall.

"Freya, that's enough!" Jarrett managed to say through clenched teeth.

She pulled back from the hole, but the FF kept rotating and still seemed to be picking up speed.

"We need help!" Agnes said.

"The Fifth Hero!" Jarrett said. "Let's grab hands, like we did before when . . ."

He'd wanted to say like we did before when we heard the Ponies talking to the Fifth Hero. But he couldn't speak another word. Being pinned to the wall made it too hard.

Luckily the others were thinking the same thing. Agnes was crawling toward Freya. Not on the floor. Along the wall. Like a spider. From the other direction, Malik was doing the same thing.

But not Jarrett. He was stuck to the wall, not just by the force of the spinning FF. His backpack was somehow hooked onto one of the exposed braces on the wall. He struggled to free himself, but he couldn't.

"Blow at me, Freya!" he shouted.

She turned her head, saw what was up, and unleashed a gust of wind that hit him like a giant rubber hammer.

"Sorry!" Freya shouted, instantly knowing she'd gone too far.

But the wind yanked Jarrett free of the crevice and sent

him flying around the rim of the FF, like a bug going down a flushing toilet. Jarrett tumbled and rolled, and then his friends caught him and they became a jumble of legs and arms.

"Got you, Jar," Agnes said. "Everyone, grab hands, quick!"

For one scary moment Jarrett realized that he was holding his own hands. Then one hand found Freya's and the other found Agnes's. They were both already connected with Malik.

There! That should do it! Jarrett waited for a flash or something and for the Ponies to start talking in that weird four-way voice. . . .

But nothing happened.

Well, something happened.

The FF fell through the air and crashed.

CHAPTER THIRTEEN

The four heroes were thrown apart and then bounced back together into a pile as the ship spun a few feet into the soft ground. As they disentangled, they all reported feeling rattled but okay. By Jarrett's count, this was the third time he'd crashed in an FF in his entire life. And all three had been in the last couple of hours.

Why hadn't the Ponies started talking to them? Maybe the Ponies were just a limited-time perk, like everything else the Calamity Corporation made?

"How far did we get in the ship before we crashed?" Malik asked.

"Ugh, I recognize that rock," Agnes said. "Maybe a hundred feet or so."

Jarrett couldn't believe it. No, it wasn't possible, was it? All that for just a hundred feet! They must have traveled straight up into the air and just spun there the whole time before dropping back down.

The ship had landed so that it faced away from the woods. Now the window gave them a clear view up the riverbed, where they'd left the family.

Much too clear. The hulking shapes of Slicer and Dicer were just now coming around the rock that jutted out into the river—the same one that had forced the heroes to wade out into the water.

Their first close-up look at the pair was even more terrifying than Jarrett thought it could be. Their arm-length blades that swirled and cut into the air as they moved looked more deadly in real life. And the blades appeared to be much sharper and stronger than they had in the hologram Lina had shown them earlier. While their bodies still bore some of the scorch marks from reentering Earth's atmosphere, the blades shone like they were brand-new.

Jarrett did spot one good thing. The robots had been designed for the low gravity of space. Up there, they were like prowling, liquid panthers, but back here on Earth they were heavier and more clunky, like bulldozers in mud. With each footstep—claw step?—they left giant divots in the shape of buckets behind them. Luckily, that seemed to slow them down a little. Every time they moved ahead, they had to pull one leg out of the hole they'd just created. As they got closer, the whirring of their blades got louder, as if they were getting hungrier.

The kids had to get out of there.

"Maybe try again, Freya?" Jarrett said. "Just use little puffs this time?"

"Okay." Freya nodded and tried blowing out the hole in the wall again. When the FuelFlighter lifted and spun this time, she was able to move the tornado so that the ship was now in the eye of the storm. It reminded Jarrett of how the family had been safer inside the whirlpool. The same thing was true here. Things were a bit steadier. And while the view out the window was just a mass of swirling dust, Jarrett could tell they were moving away from Slicer and Dicer, and quickly.

"What direction do we want to go in?" Malik asked.

Jarrett squinted out the window. He could barely make out a small yellow disk high in the sky through all the debris. "That's the sun, so that's what? West, right? Go that way!"

With a shake of her head, Freya said, "I can't exactly steer this thing." She tried releasing just a puff, and then another. Then the FF turned in the direction of the sun. "Huh, maybe I can control it after all."

"Way to go, Freya!" Jarrett said, and they all found spots on the floor to settle in.

Every minute or so Freya blew through her hand to keep the tornado spinning and the FF flying through the air. It was hard to say, but Jarrett guessed the Climate Club had already traveled a couple hundred miles. Then, after about twenty-five minutes, a jolt ran through the FF, and it dipped toward the ground.

"Oops," Freya said.

"Oops?" Jarrett asked, alarmed.

"I think my battery or whatever is running low," Freya explained. She held up her hand so they could see it. The green sphere there was almost completely dark, as if it had been drained of power.

"Can you land us?" Agnes asked.

"I don't know if I have enough juice left, but I can try."

She leaned back toward the hole, but this time when she blew through it, their speed didn't change. In fact, the FF had slowed down. As if to explain what was happening, Freya held out her hand again. It was totally dark now. The FF spun again, but not as violently, and then with a massive jolt they hit the ground. The crash knocked the hatch open.

"Nice landing, Freya, you know, considering," Jarrett said, and they all agreed.

"Thanks," Freya said.

As they had earlier, Freya and Jarrett went to the hatch. This time they pushed instead of pulled. And before long, warm air and sand was blowing into the FF through the open door.

"We're at the beach!" Agnes shouted. "I love the beach!"

"No," Malik said. "This is the desert."

"How do you know?" Agnes challenged him.

"Um, because there's no water," he said.

Agnes rolled her eyes and laughed. "Okay, okay, good point. But what are the odds? I mean, we need to get to the finish line in the desert, and suddenly we're in a desert?"

"It makes you wonder if somehow these things are nudging us where to go," Jarrett said, holding up his hand with the sphere.

"Yes, these things," Agnes said. "Or maybe the Fifth Hero?"

"Well, we haven't been nudged to the finish line yet," Jarrett said. "When we first saw the robots, they looked like they might have been flying. But maybe they were just falling out of orbit."

Jarrett hoped the latter was the case. Because if the robots could take off and fly whenever they wanted, that meant they could be right behind the kids. Either way, they had to get out of this FF.

But Malik said, "We can't just run off into a desert!"

"We won't have to!" Agnes said, pulling him over to the window. "Look, that's a cave!"

They all went to check out the view. About a hundred feet away there was indeed a small opening in the side of a rocky hill. Jarrett's gut told him that was the last place they wanted to go.

"Where there's a way in, there must be another way out," Agnes said. "In all the movies, the heroes go into a cave and discover it's actually a long tunnel. They always come out on the other side, right where they wanted to go all along."

Jarrett was tempted to tell Agnes that this wasn't a movie. This was *nature*. But Slicer and Dicer weren't exactly keeping their options open. So he just shrugged. "What choice do we have?"

Everyone nodded, and they very carefully poked their heads out of the FF's hatch. The dust was still settling, but they could see up into the sky. There was no sign of flying robots, for now. With Agnes in the front, they hurried to the entrance of the cave.

Immediately, Jarrett's nostrils were hit by the foulest stench. What horrible creature called *this* place home?

Toward the back of the cave, the passage narrowed into yet another hole that led deeper into the rocky hill. Malik's and Freya's Ponies were both dark now, so Jarrett and Agnes held up their palms like flashlights to get a better look. But the light seemed to be eaten up by the darkness, and it was hard to tell where it might take them.

"Why would we want to find out what's in here?" Jarrett asked.

"Because we know what's out there," Agnes said, gesturing back toward the exit.

"Fine," Jarrett said, and they pushed ahead.

The four kids skidded down a slippery slope and found themselves standing at the bottom in deep piles of muck. The smell! This is where the stench was coming from. And there were chittering noises. Jarrett looked up. The ceiling was covered with some kind of black cloth that billowed as if wind were blowing through it. But there was no wind. And there was no cloth.

Jarrett's beam didn't show quite as much detail as Agnes's ultra-bright one, but as he moved his light from the slick walls of the cave and pointed it straight up overhead, he could see that the ceiling was covered with thousands and thousands of wriggling, squeaking upside-down creatures.

Oh no.

They were in a cave filled with bats.

CHAPTER FOURTEEN

It was like a painting that Jarrett had seen in a museum a couple of years ago. From far away you couldn't tell that the painting of old-timey people in a park had a secret. As you got closer though, you could see the image was made of thousands of little dots. Here, it was the same thing. The ceiling rose and fell like the black surface of water at night, with rolling waves of movement. But if he hovered the light on his palm over one spot, he could make out a single creature about the size of a large banana hanging upside down and stirring slightly in its sleep.

He dropped his hand. He closed his eyes. This. This. This was terrifying.

Then something wriggled up his arm—

His eyes flew open. It was only Agnes patting his shoulder. "You okay there, Jar?" she asked. But she was busy looking up and running the light from her hand over the ceiling.

"You know what this place is?" Malik asked quietly.

"A nightmare?" Jarrett said.

"It's a cave, Jar," Agnes said, chuckling. "And it's full of bats. And they are so cute!"

"No," Malik corrected her. "This is our ticket home. Everyone thinks this kind of long-nosed bat is almost extinct. The other racers are out there catching one or two at a time. We've got thousands here! We can close up the entrance to the cave and trap them all inside. With all these bats, we can win the race!"

Still gazing up at the squirming masses, Agnes seemed unsure. "I don't know, Malik."

"What don't you know?" he shot back. "If we win the race, the world will be watching, and Tommy can't possibly do anything bad to us. He'll have to call off Slicer and Dicer. Plus, we'll win the Grand Prize—we'll get off Earth!"

Not looking convinced, Freya said, "But . . . well, no."

It was a long speech for Freya, and Jarrett nodded. "Freya is right. If we go outside to seal the cave, Slicer and Dicer will get us. And if we seal it from the inside, we'll be trapped in here too."

"You don't get it!" As if tired of arguing, Malik hurried

over to a spot where the cave ceiling was especially low. He jumped and used the back of his hand to try to knock down one of the bats.

"Don't do that," Freya said, and Agnes stepped toward Malik to stop him.

"There must be another way," Agnes said. "They're . . . alive, Malik. We shouldn't hurt them."

But Malik didn't listen. He jumped and swung his hand in the air again. This time he connected with a bat. It fell to the squishy ground, where it squiggled frantically on its side, letting out sad little chirps.

"There!" Malik cried triumphantly. "Got one!"

The chirping was getting even more high-pitched, as if begging someone to *please, please listen.* Jarrett told himself not to, but he touched his ear with the fingers of his glowing hand. The cards that flew from the bat in front of him didn't make any sense. They were just dark colors mixed with panicky squeaks.

Jarrett took his hand away. He couldn't look at the cards. They were even scarier than the billowing ceiling. Who knew he could be so moved by one of these scary, bitey creatures?

Almost without thinking, he touched his palm to his throat and said, "It's okay. You're going to be okay." Two cards, one with a water drop and the other with what looked like a mosquito, flew from his mouth into the air and hung over the bat. But was it too late? Other than a little twitch of its nose, the bat had gone still, with one of its wings bent at a weird angle.

Had it been knocked unconscious? Was it all right? It was hard to say.

"One down," Malik crowed. He stepped under another group of bats. "Now just about a million more to go."

A million? Jarrett didn't think he could stand even one more. The sounds were just so sad.

"Malik, stop!" Agnes cried. "Look, now even its little nose has stopped twitching!"

"Good, right?" Malik said, but he didn't sound completely sure of himself anymore. Jarrett could see he wouldn't—or couldn't—look at the little bat on the ground. "That's one less pest to worry about. I did us all a big favor. You're welcome."

As Malik reached up to knock down another bat, Jarrett made a split-second decision. He put his hand to his throat and shouted as loud as he'd ever shouted.

"RUN!"

Jarrett put every drop of his energy and strength into that one single word. The card that left his lips hung heavily in front of him. It was the size of a classroom smartboard and on it was the image of a stick figure running.

In that instant, Jarrett thought, *Run? Why did I say that? Bats can't run.*

With his free hand, he gave the card a good whack. It spun once and then cracked apart into more than a hundred smaller pieces. All little copies of the larger card, they continued spinning as they fanned out across the cave. Then, like an incredible fireworks display, they all exploded at once with a blinding violet light.

The word *run* might not be in their vocabulary, but the bats got the idea. The tiny explosions woke them. Instantly, the thousands and thousands of bats let go of their perches on the ceiling, their wings flapping, their bodies jerking into motion. They bumped up against each other as they swarmed toward the cave's exit, trying desperately to get outside. Their little bodies and claws were just inches away from the kids' faces, and sometimes not even inches.

"Ahhhh!" Jarrett yelled. He dropped to the ground after ten or so bats bounced off him—the breeze and the sound created by their wings was terrifying. Agnes threw herself to the ground too. Malik went down into a crouch, with hands up and protecting his face. Several bats got snagged in Freya's piled-high hair, but she calmly reached up and freed them.

Then the cave was quiet. The only light left came from Agnes's palm. Jarrett's Pony was now dark. He must have used up all its power.

"Why did you do that, Jarrett?" Malik demanded.

Jarrett ignored him. Next to him, Agnes was breathing

heavily. She and Jarrett were covered in bat guano from dropping to the ground. They both shook their arms, trying to get the soupy, stinky stuff off.

"You okay, Aggie?" Jarrett asked.

"This was a bad idea," Agnes said, and moved the reddish light coming from her palm over the now-empty ceiling and the solid walls of the cave. It was like watching the beam from a lighthouse cutting through the fog. There were no other ways out of the cave.

"It's a dead end," she said. "I don't get it. In all the adventure movies, the heroes always find a secret passage back to the surface."

"But . . . ," Jarrett started to say, and then stopped. He was too tired to keep reminding her about what nature really was.

". . . this isn't a movie," Agnes finished his sentence for him. "I'm sorry, guys."

"It's okay, Agnes." Jarrett had crouched down over the limp body of the bat. It was the only one left in the cave. "We need to get help for this guy," he said.

"Why? Where? How?" Malik demanded.

Jarrett didn't know how to answer any of those questions. "All I know is we need to get out of here."

"Slicer and Dicer are out there!" Malik protested.

"But soon they'll be in here," Freya said. "Bats don't leave their nests till evening normally. The robots will see the swarm of bats leaving the cave early and know that something scared them off."

It was the most words any of them had ever heard her string together. And those words hit home.

Agnes said, "They'll come into the cave to investigate."

"And we'll have nowhere to run," Jarrett completed the thought.

"Come," Freya said. And no one made a joke about Freya talking to them like they were dogs. Things were way too real for that. With Freya right behind her, Agnes led the way up the steep slope to the passageway that would take them back outside. Malik and Jarrett brought up the rear. But not before Jarrett took a second to put the fragile bat carefully into his backpack.

In just seconds, Freya and Agnes had scrambled up the slick incline on their hands and knees and waited for the boys at the top. Agnes shone her Pony light down on Jarrett and Malik so they could make their way up too.

As they crawled up, Malik gave Jarrett's shoulder a swat.

"Hey!" Jarrett said defensively. "Don't hit me! I'm not a bat!"

"Oh, come on, I tapped you," Malik shot back.

"Okay, why did you *tap* me, Malik?"

"We could've won the race."

"We're not trying to win the race, remember?" Jarrett sighed.

"But what a great bonus it'd be to win a trip to space!" Malik practically shouted. "What's with you and those bats, Jarrett?"

Jarrett shivered. "You can't hear what I can hear. It's horrible."

"Okay," Malik said. "I mean, it just seems like you warned the bats to get back at me or something. I thought we were friends. I thought we liked each other."

Jarrett stopped climbing. Was Malik for real? "We haven't talked since everything with Jarma. After you dumped me as your science class partner. Is that the way friends act?"

Even in the dark, Jarrett could tell Malik's face was flushed. He had stopped climbing too. After a pause, he said, "We've had some dangerous stuff to deal with. Tommy and his robots are out to get us. Sometimes it feels like the whole planet is after us."

"I'm starting to think Earth might not be as bad as we thought," Jarrett muttered.

"Is that why you saved the bats?" Malik asked. "Because you think they're good?"

"Maybe, and because it was the right thing to do," Jarrett fired back. "I think a lot of people would have done what I did back there. If they had the right information, they'd do the right thing too."

"Come on!" Freya called to the boys. But Agnes hushed her. "They have things to figure out."

"I know what's happening here," Malik said to Jarrett. "You've cleaned up a tiny corner of your room." He started climbing again.

"What's that mean?" Jarrett asked.

"I feel better when I clean up my room and it's all done. But then, guess what. It's dirty again in about five seconds," Malik said. "What's the point?"

"It's a good five seconds, though, isn't it, Malik?"

"I'm not saying this right. I'm good at coming up with games, not talking about all this serious stuff."

"Try," Jarrett said.

Malik took a breath. "Okay. Think about it like this. When I make my bed, how does that make me feel?"

"Like you've accomplished something?"

"No, in a very big way, it makes me feel bad," Malik answered. "Because then everything else in my room looks super messy. It's like, once you start cleaning, you suddenly realize you have to clean everything, not just that one spot, and it seems sort of hopeless. Like, why bother? Isn't it easier to just not do anything?"

Jarrett couldn't believe what he was hearing. "It sounds

kind of like you're saying that instead of making our beds we should just move to a new house. You want to give up on Earth because you don't want to be bothered to clean it!"

"Well," Malik said, his face losing some of its anger. "When you put it like that . . ."

But Jarrett wasn't listening anymore. It was infuriating. How could someone he cared about be so wasteful? "I don't know what else to tell you, Malik," Jarrett announced as he reached the top of the ramp. "Other than I'm calling this little guy Jarma II."

"Jarma II?" Freya asked. Her long red hair had fallen out of the pile and was a wild wave behind her. "Who's that?"

"This bat." Jarrett unslung his backpack gently and unzipped it. Lying on top of the birthday banner as if it were a nest was Jarma, one wing still bent at the side.

"Oh, he's so . . . ," Agnes said.

"Cute? I guess," Jarrett. He just wished bats weren't so scary too.

"Is he alive?" Freya asked.

"He's breathing," Jarrett said. "Or at least, I think he is. I'm going to take him to an animal doctor. I'm not collecting or hunting him." He looked at Malik, who had joined them by now. "Like some people do."

Malik looked away.

"I bet all's fine," Freya said. "Nature is so—"

"Resilient?" Jarrett asked, losing his temper again. "Does he look like a toy you'd win at the carnival? Or like something that can snap back with no problem no matter what we do to him?"

"You might want to dial it down, Jar," Agnes said.

She was right. Jarrett was mad at Malik and he was taking it out on Freya and Agnes. "Sorry, guys, let's just get out of here."

As the four emerged from the cave, squinting against the blazing sun of the late afternoon, they discussed their next move.

"We need to somehow find the finish line," Agnes said. "If we don't get there by dark, Lina's parents will be gone. If they leave, we'll never track them down. I mean, their own kids can't find them for more than ten seconds at a time."

"Speaking of finding things," Malik said, "it looks like Slicer and Dicer found our FF."

The Climate Club stared in shock at the FuelFlighter. Or what was left of it. It had been torn to shreds. The thick metal walls had been ripped apart like toilet paper.

Jarrett felt unsteady. "The robots can't be far away."

"You're right," Freya said quietly. "They're right there."

CHAPTER FIFTEEN

Slicer and Dicer poked up from behind the wreckage of the FF, as if they'd been hiding there, just waiting. The high-pitched whine of the robot's machinery reminded Jarrett of a dentist's drill . . . only it sounded hungrier. And black exhaust billowed from four different pipes on each robot, creating a putrid, smoky fog around them.

Malik was the first to move. "Back into the cave! Quick!"

"No!" Agnes said.

"We have to get inside," Jarrett said. "We can't fight them. Our Ponies are out of juice."

"Mine isn't," Agnes protested.

"But you don't even know what yours does!" Jarrett shouted.

"Agnes is right," Freya said. "They'll follow us into the cave."

"We'll be trapped!" Agnes's voice had reached that breaking point again. "I was wrong about going in there before. The robots destroy asteroids. They'd tear through that cave with no problem!"

"So where can we go?" Malik said. He was throwing rocks at the robots, but they just obliterated them with their slicing and dicing blades. "We're in the middle of nowhere, and we have no choice!"

"No, I'm not going into that cave!" Like a toddler refusing to go an inch farther, Agnes dropped to her knees and put her hands onto the hard-packed sand. "This isn't fair!"

"Agnes, fair doesn't matter," Jarrett said. "There isn't a referee we can call. This isn't a game."

"I know it's not a game," she insisted, but Jarrett wondered if she really did.

The robots were lumbering closer and closer to them, and Agnes shouted, "I am so tired of being afraid of you!" As if to emphasize her emotion, she lifted her hands and slammed them both down on the ground.

BOOM! It was like someone had dropped a hammer on a giant drum . . . from three stories up. The earth shook.

Everyone, including Slicer and Dicer, froze.

Agnes looked down at her hands. "Whoa," she said. "I think I just found my power."

The whine of machinery reached a new pitch as the robots jerked into motion again, this time coming at the kids more quickly.

"Not so fast," Agnes said, and she slammed her palm with the sphere down again. A small crack opened in the earth between her hands.

With a jolt of realization, Jarrett remembered why the Ponies had been created in the first place. Tommy had made them to destroy Earth and its climate. Was Agnes helping that happen? Was she about to tear the world apart?

"Uh, you might want to ease back, Aggie," he warned her.

"No way, no how," she said. "I'm way too mad." She brought her hands down again. Now the split in the ground snaked away from Agnes and wove its way out into the desert.

Glancing back, Agnes tried reassuring them. "Don't worry, I think I can kind of control this."

Kind of? Jarrett thought.

"I won't hurt anything," Agnes continued. "Well, maybe one or *two* things."

Turning her attention back to the robots, she connected her hands to the sand once more. **WHAM!** The split made a sharp turn in the general direction of the robots.

She tapped the sand more lightly, and now the split was on a direct course for the robots. "I've got the hang of it now," Jarrett heard Agnes say.

Slicer and Dicer were busily destroying the rocks that were being thrown their way and didn't notice when the split wormed its way between them and continued on.

"One, two, three . . . hold on," Agnes warned her friends. She stood up and jumped in the air and brought her hands down onto the ground with the biggest connection yet.

It was like watching a golf ball move through a long sock. Jarrett could see the power traveling from her hands along the split until it reached the robots and then—

KAKLAM! The split burst open like a seam. It opened wider and wider until it had gone under the clawed feet of the unsuspecting robots. Slicer tried firing his rockets, and then so did Dicer, hoping to blast off. But there wasn't any ground below them, and it was too late.

They tumbled into the hole. They crashed into each other with an enormous, eardrum-shattering bang. Then they disappeared.

"Yes!" Jarrett shouted. "Yes!"

But the hole kept expanding. . . . It was still getting wider—

"Uh-oh," Agnes said. "There's a bunch of tunnels or something down there. I'm having a tough time closing it all up!"

Gently but with urgency, Agnes brought her hands closer together and made smoothing motions on the sand with her palms. The effect was immediate. The split started to heal and fade away. The healing continued along the split at lightning speed, moving away from Agnes. Finally, only the giant hole was left, and Agnes used more force as she filled that in as well. In a flash, the ground there came together, burying Slicer and Dicer below.

Agnes kept smoothing the sand—the hole with Slicer and Dicer had almost disappeared—until all that was left was an indentation a couple of inches deep. Agnes seemed determined to completely fix the ground, but nothing further happened. She lifted her hand and showed the others—it was dark. She'd used up all the Ponies' power.

She leapt to her feet, grinning, and, without thinking, they all reached out to each other to celebrate—

Freya was saying to Agnes, "How amazing are—"

—when their hands connected with a flash of light.

QUICK! TURN TO PAGE 187!

CHAPTER EIGHTEEN

"**O**f course, it's me," the voice said, and then added, "you big dummy."

Okay, Jarrett thought. No doubt about it now. This was Lina.

"Why did you run away from that spot in the woods?" Lina demanded. It was unnerving to hear her voice coming out of Slidicer's mouth. "You guys aren't actually trying to win the race, are you? You don't want Tommy to know anything more about you than he already does! He just flew off in his FF, probably coming to pick you guys up, so I'm in my FF right behind him."

Jarrett realized that everyone had frozen to listen to Lina, even Slidicer. Its head was tilted to one side like a dog who doesn't understand a command.

"Don't worry," Lina said, as if sensing their confusion. "I've been able to freeze Slicer's and Dicer's bodies for now, and I've taken over their voice systems." Then she paused. They could hear her moving around. "But I can't override the controls forever," she continued. "The security mechanism will kick me out at some point. I'm surprised I could get in at all! Did something happen to them?"

Agnes was stunned. "You could say that. . . ."

"Well, they were showing up on the map until just a bit ago," Lina said. "You didn't hurt them, did you?"

Malik took a step back as if he couldn't believe his ears. "What did you say?"

"You'd better not have done anything drastic," Lina said.

Right then, Slidicer picked up a rock and began banging it against his head, as if trying to make Lina stop talking.

"What's that noise?" Lina asked. "Are you guys hitting one of the robots? Do you know how expensive Slicer and Dicer are? Are you trying to add trillions more to the trillions you already owe my family? Not to mention how epically catastrophic you've already made my birthday!"

"Money? All you care about is money?!" Malik yelled. "You should be asking if *they* have hurt *us*! We've been running for our lives all day from these two."

For the first time all day Malik's voice didn't sound incredibly fake when he was talking to Lina. He finally sounded real. And Jarrett loved it.

"Okay, okay," Lina said. "Well, just so you know you'll want to keep your distance from them."

"They're the ones who won't keep their distance from us, Lina!" Jarrett shouted.

Maybe it was finally getting to Lina that they were in real danger. She took in a breath. "Well, *if* that's true, you'll never beat them in a fight, you know. I can only keep them where they are for about another minute. You'll need to turn the robots off manually to prevent them from following you."

Forcing himself to remain as calm as possible, Jarrett said, "Lina. We're in big trouble. Please just tell us how to stop the robot."

"Wow, guys, so pushy," Lina said. "You can be a little more appreciative, I think. Why did you guys have to try to save the planet in the first place?"

"We're appreciative!" Agnes shouted.

"Relax," Lina said. "I'm just kidding! Kind of. There are two wires on the back on all of Calamity Corp's asteroid smashers. One red, one blue. I can see they're still intact on my control panel, but I can't deactivate them from here. If you cut the wrong wire, the robots will self-destruct in an explosion that will wipe out everything within a mile. Also, you have thirty seconds. Well, twenty-eight now . . ."

"Hurry up, Lina!" Jarrett shouted.

"Oh, now I can't hear you either," Lina said. "Hmm . . . the listening systems have gone dark."

"Just tell us which wire to cut!" Freya yelled.

"Anyway," Lina continued calmly, clearly unable to hear Freya, "if you can hear me, no matter which wire you cut, you'll shut down the weaponry. But seriously, whatever you do, the *blue* wire—"

Having tried everything else, Slidicer reached up and sliced out its own voice box. The robot held the device out and crushed it in its hand. The wiring popped, sizzled, and smoked.

All four kids stared at the robot, stunned.

"Uh, now what?" Jarrett asked.

CHAPTER NINETEEN

"Which wire do we cut?" Agnes demanded. "Did she say the blue one?"

"I don't know, but I think so," Jarrett said. "Why couldn't Lina have just told us when she had the chance?"

The Climate Club circled the robot, looking for an opening through the swirling blades. Slidicer spun its head, watching them furiously with its fiery eyes.

"I've played enough video games to know how to beat the bad guy at the end of a level," Malik said. "I think there's a pattern to the slicing of the blades. Yes! I see it. There's a way. But we're all too big. We couldn't squeeze through the opening without getting cut."

"Sounds like we might need a little help, Jarrett," Agnes said.

Understanding what she meant, Jarrett put his hands up to his mouth to create a kind of megaphone. And he shouted, "Who can cut something for us? Please. Thanks! Oh, and just so you know, it's rather dangerous!" Cards flew out of his mouth and up into the air, down into the ground, and went skittering off toward the horizon.

"*Rather* dangerous? Please? Thanks?" Agnes scoffed. "Why are you talking so formally?"

Jarrett shrugged. "Just trying to be polite, I guess."

Two vultures flew overhead, just out of reach of Slidicer's blades, and started circling there. They seemed to make Slidicer even angrier, and he turned his attention to them.

"Did you call those vultures?" Malik asked. "Or do they think they're going to get dinner?"

Jarrett put his hand to his ear and saw cards with images of what looked like intestines.

"Um, the second option," Jarrett answered.

Seconds later, cards with weird symbols popped up everywhere. The replies to his request were finally coming in. Jarrett had never known even a desert could be filled with so much life.

A card flew up from the ground directly in front of Jarret. He glanced down and shouted, "Ah!"

He jumped back.

A scorpion about six inches long was at their feet. It skittered at the sudden movement from Jarrett, and its stinger tail bobbed up and down a bit, but it stood its ground.

"I can't see the 'cards' you keep talking about, Jar," Agnes said. "But if I had to guess, I'd say this scorpion is saying hi and volunteering his services."

Getting a grip, Jarrett spoke through his hand to the scorpion. "Hello. Can you help us? Please cut the blue wire on the right. But if we do it wrong, *boom*!"

A card with a bunch of black lines popped up from the scorpion. What'd that mean? Jarrett wondered. Maybe confusion? Too late to find out. The scorpion rushed over to Slidicer.

"Are we really relying on a scorpion to save us?" Malik asked doubtfully.

"Don't worry, they're tough," Freya said. "Scorpions can survive without their tails, and they can survive being frozen."

Agnes looked surprised. "How do you know that?"

Freya shrugged. "I like scorpions," she said. "When you live with your grandparents in the middle of nowhere, you can wind up with interesting pets."

Slidicer didn't notice the scorpion skittering along the sand and up his back. The robot was too busy flailing at the birds circling overhead.

"Hold on, something about this doesn't feel right," Freya said.

"Really?" Jarrett asked her, and then checked in with the scorpion by talking through his hand. "Are you doing okay?"

The cards he got in response from the scorpion seemed wrong somehow. "It's the weirdest thing," Jarrett said. "The cards all look backward. Like a reflection."

"That actually makes sense," Freya said. "Scorpions can have twelve eyes, two in front and five on each side. But the eyes don't do much. Scorpions mostly 'see' by feeling vibrations with little hairs on their bodies. So they can't see colors."

"That's okay," Jarrett said. "I told him to cut the wire on the right. And that's the blue one."

"No, it's not okay," Freya insisted. "If scorpions see with their bodies, their idea of right and left could be different from our right and left. It could be the opposite!"

"Oh no," Malik said. "Right could be left, and left could be right."

It hit Jarrett like a punch: the scorpion could be about to cut the wrong wire.

"Wait!" he shouted, and a card flew out of his mouth. But he was too late.

Snip!

The scorpion sliced the blue wire with its pincer, and, with a wave of its tail, it scuttled off into a hole in the ground.

For a moment nothing happened. Then Slidicer's four blades lowered.

"Whew," Jarrett said. "Maybe that did the trick—"

Slidicer's head flew up and the whirring reached new heights, now joined by beeps.

It was clear that the beeps were a countdown of some kind, and they were getting closer and closer to each other. Jarrett figured that when there was no more space between the beeps the robots would self-destruct.

"If what Lina said about the explosion wiping everything out for a mile was true, we can't outrun it," Malik said. "And the finish line is somewhere nearby. We won't be the only ones to get . . ."

"Blown up?" Agnes suggested.

Malik nodded.

"Can you bring a hurricane or something, Freya?" Jarrett asked. "You could fling Slidicer away."

Freya held up her palm. "I don't think so. The air doesn't feel right. And Slidicer is too heavy for me to just blow it a mile away. But maybe I can do this. . . ."

She waved her palm in the air, and the result was instant. A sandstorm about the width of a small swimming pool rose up out of the desert at Slidicer's feet. Freya struggled for a bit as the storm engulfed the kids and blinded them with flinging dust. She changed the motion of her hands, and the storm became more contained as it spun around Slidicer. But it was still just loose sand that wouldn't do much to stop the robot from blowing up!

Then, suddenly, Slidicer was moving. It was only a couple of feet every five seconds or so, but it was moving toward them. The message was clear: if it was going to go, it was going to take them all with it.

"Can you try shaking it up, Aggie?" Jarrett asked.

"You mean like an airquake instead of an earthquake?" Agnes put her hands up and pushed against the air. "I can't get a grip on anything."

"Maybe I can help," Malik offered. He put his palm down. "I can feel a little water under here. Hold on." He pulled up a thin sheet of water that rose between them and Slidicer, but the robot just walked right through it. The sand on its body became a coating of mud.

"Sorry, guys, my power isn't exactly the strongest in the desert," Malik said.

But Agnes seemed excited. "Oh, don't be sorry. I can work with this."

And, with her hands in front of her, Agnes ran toward Slidicer.

"No!" Before Jarrett could think about it, he was grabbing his friend by the back of her shirt. He tried pulling her away from the robot, but her momentum carried them both forward, until they were only a few feet from the robot.

"Who's the one taking chances now?" she asked with a grin.

Beepbeepbeepbeep.

The beeping was almost one solid sound now with no breaks in between. Slidicer would self-destruct in seconds.

Jarrett said, "Please, can you just . . . not . . . be . . . so . . . you!"

"Ha, I don't think so," Agnes said. "Don't let me get dragged in." Jarrett nodded, and Agnes put her palm out to touch the robot. When she connected with the metal creature, the mud coating instantly began to move. She packed the mud around Slidicer like a cement cocoon until the robot couldn't move anymore.

Agnes brought her hand away. Jarrett could see the cocoon start to crack. It would fall apart in seconds without Agnes holding it in place—

"Get back!" she shouted, and pushed him toward Freya and Malik, following right behind.

BAM!

CHAPTER TWENTY

The massive explosion rippled inside the sand casing like a wild animal trapped in a pillowcase. It clawed to get free for a few moments. Then—**BFFT!**—chunks of hardened sand burst out from the center of the casing. Clumps of it blasted over the Climate Club's heads, followed by waves of heat that singed Jarrett's nose hairs. The explosion pushed the friends back a few inches, but they all managed to stay on their feet.

The remaining casing collapsed onto the ground like a sheet falling from a clothesline. Smoking bits of metal smoldered in the pile of sizzling, wet sand. But there were no more terrifying beeps, no more creepy wires crackling, and best of all . . . no more scary red eyes.

Slidicer had been destroyed!

Still, all four kids stayed ready to leap into action. They had spent so long either fleeing from or fighting the robots, it was hard to relax even a bit. Then, finally, the Climate Club started to breathe normally again. They all turned to one another, stunned but happy.

"I can't believe it," Jarrett said, feeling like they should high-five or something to celebrate. "We just defeated space robots with our superpowers."

Grinning, Agnes chuckled softly. Then stopped. "Do you think Slidicer is really dead?"

With a shrug, Malik answered, "I hope so, but in all the horror movies, this is when the bad guys pop back up to surprise everyone."

Freya must have seen the same movies, because she shuddered. "We'd better keep moving," she said. "The finish line is right over that sand dune."

With Freya leading the way, the friends backed away from the wreckage of Slidicer and started climbing up the nearby dune. It was at least the height of a three-story building, making it a tough slog up the sliding sand.

"I'm empty." Malik tapped the dark sphere in his palm. He sounded a little winded from the steep climb. "How about everyone else?"

Freya and Agnes nodded. Their palms were dark too. It

had taken everything the Club had to defeat Slidicer. But there was still a tiny flicker of light in Jarrett's palm.

"Should I use up my power so we can recharge?" Jarrett wondered, panting from the exertion. "We still might need the power and maybe some help from the Fifth Hero."

"We don't have time," Malik said. "The sun's about to go down."

Jarrett nodded. "If Lina's parents leave before we get there, we won't be able to find anyone who can help us. Plus, the Ponies might be easier to take out of our hands when they're empty."

The others agreed, and they hurried up the rest of the sand dune. At the top, the friends finally got what they had fought for all day . . . a view of the finish line. Below them, in a valley between three tall dunes, there was a stage with a curtain and a crowd of at least three hundred people. Teams of competitors mingled and milled about under bright overhead lights, all carrying bags of popcorn or bowls of ice cream. It was a giant party.

"Wow, I guess we're not the first ones to get to the finish line," Jarrett murmured.

"Nowhere near the first," Agnes agreed.

Many in the crowd had captured long-nosed bats. The frightened, chittering animals were imprisoned in floating cages that bobbed over the crowd like huge party balloons.

Jarrett was tempted to put his hand to his ear to listen to what the bats were saying. But he didn't think he could bear hearing their cries for help.

"Oh, wow," Malik said, gesturing toward the back of the crowd. "Look at that!"

Jarrett did a double take. "Is that a bouncy house?"

But the answer was an obvious yes. Even from up here, he could hear people hooting and laughing inside the giant inflatable room. A banner hung over the entrance to the bouncy house, and it read ENTER TO STOMP OUT something. From this angle, Jarrett couldn't see the whole slogan. On both sides of the crowd, concession stands were handing out hot dogs and snacks. And next to the stage was a square building that reminded Jarret of an enormous garden shed. That had a sign, too, and it read FURNACE. DEPOSIT YOUR PESTS HERE!

"Oh no," Agnes said, looking past Jarrett's shoulder at the sun, which had almost completely disappeared over the horizon. "The Limwicks said they'd be here at sunset. Are we too late?"

Jarrett didn't know, but he wanted to shout at the sun to go the other way, as if it would listen.

"Come on," Freya commanded. They tumbled down the sand dune toward the gathering of people. Jarrett was careful not to crush the fragile cargo in his backpack. At the bottom, the club finally stumbled to a stop in front of a family of six who were dressed in matching red survival jumpsuits. One was a curly-haired boy, maybe twelve or thirteen. In one hand, he held a thick string that led up to a floating cage of bats, and he had tears streaming down his cheeks.

Before Jarrett could ask what was wrong, the boy moaned, "We just needed to catch two more! Two more bats and we could have beaten them and won the race!"

The boy pointed at three teenaged girls who had identical glittery tiaras on their heads. They were bouncing a trophy that was nearly as big as Jarrett. It was made of two interlocking *C*s, which stood for Calamity Corporation, wrapped around each other like snakes. The girls shouted triumphantly into drone cameras that swarmed all around them, "We won the Race to Erase! And now we get to go to space!"

Obviously, the Climate Club was too late for the award ceremony. "Did we miss Lina's parents too?" Jarrett said. "Are they gone?"

They scanned the crowd and the stage. No sign of the Limwicks. But Jarrett noticed many of the other teams had dressed in matching costumes to take part in the race, and the Climate Club wasn't the only group wearing masks.

"There they are!" Freya cried. "On the stage!"

She was right. Decked out in matching bright pink jackets and white pants, the Doctors Limwick had just walked out onto the stage. As Lina's parents waved, the crowd clapped and cheered as though the couple were the world's biggest rock stars. After a few deep bows, the doctors held out their hands for quiet, clearly about to give a speech.

"Yes!" Jarrett said, relieved that their struggles to get here hadn't been for nothing. "Now we just need them to help us. Let's go!"

Together the Climate Club rushed toward the stage. Jarrett was already planning what he would say to the Limwicks. But the friends didn't get far. There was a line of security guards wearing Calamity Corporation uniforms in front of the stage. The guards waved Jarrett and the others back—and the looks on their faces showed they meant business. This approach wasn't going to work.

Agnes pulled the club away from the stage and over to the center of the audience. "Let's just wait here," she said. "We'll get the Limwicks' attention once their speech is over."

"Shhh!" a nearby woman hushed them, and the Climate Club quieted down as the Limwicks started to speak.

"Congratulations again to our winners of today's Race to Erase!" Lina's dad said from the stage, in his deep voice. The three winning girls hooted from the back of the crowd, and there was a smattering of applause from the audience.

"Before we destroy the pests that you've all captured in the furnace," Dr. Limwick continued, "we'd like to thank you for coming to this horrible place. We promise not to keep you outside for too long. If anyone starts to feel sick from Outside-ness, please let us know."

Other than being anxious, Jarrett realized he felt fine. Not for the first time that day, he wondered if being outside was really as dangerous as everyone said.

Lina's mom stepped forward to take over the speech. "You might be curious why we chose this place as the finish for this Race to Erase. Well, now it's time to show you. A quick warning, what you are about to see is very disturbing."

With that, the huge curtain behind the Limwicks dropped, revealing twenty prickly-looking plants growing out of the sandy ground behind the stage.

"Wow," Freya said. "Those desert cactuses are super rare."

To Jarrett's surprise, the crowd booed and hissed at the six-foot-tall cactuses. *I mean,* he thought, *I'm not too comfortable with nature, but booing plants?* That just seemed over the top. As the crowd continued to yell at the plants, the sun disappeared completely. Then, as if a switch had been thrown, a white blossom started to open on one of the cactuses.

"Disgusting, right?" Lina's mom shuddered, pointing at the blossom. "I warned you it would be disturbing."

Touching his stomach as if he felt queasy, Lina's dad said, "This plant is just one symbol of Earth's failures. These flowers blossom only *once* a year—at *night*, when all good things should be asleep. They're worn out, just like everything else on this planet. Not to worry, though! The Calamity Corporation will fix this calamity just like we have time and time again."

With a smile, Lina's mom said, "This plant needs the bats you have captured to survive. By imprisoning those awful flying pests, you've prevented the pollinating of this weak plant and it will die. Now our corporation can build new things that will be so much better. We'll invent new plants and new creatures. All will be strong and beautiful in our new home in space."

What? Jarrett's mind reeled. So much of what she said didn't sound right. But people around them were clapping. Before Jarrett could speak, though, Malik beat him to the punch. He called out, "You can make something more beautiful than that flower?" Malik's voice sounded uncertain, like he had just heard two plus two equals five.

Jarrett was glad Malik had spoken up, but there was an angry murmur from the crowd. People didn't like anyone interrupting the Limwicks, and the Limwicks weren't having it either.

"Of course we can manufacture something better," Lina's mom said. "Calamity Corporation will make all the plants you'll ever need. Now, back to our speech . . ."

As the Limwicks kept talking, Malik took Jarrett's hand.

"You were right, Jarrett," Malik told him. "Maybe Earth isn't as bad as they keep telling us, and this is all wrong."

Jarrett felt a surge of hope. If Jarrett and Malik could change their minds about nature and the future of Earth, maybe other people could. Still holding on to Malik's hand, Jarrett turned to the people around them and said, "Hi, everyone! My friends and I have seen things in nature today—"

A group of eight men all wearing the same college sweatshirts shushed him.

But Jarrett kept talking. "—and what the Limwicks are saying doesn't make sense!"

As the shushing spread through the nearby crowd, Agnes and Freya stepped protectively closer to Malik and Jarrett. But the Limwicks seemed interested in the commotion, and Lina's dad put up a hand in a calming gesture. "No, no, let those strange, masked children speak," he said. "We always love to hear from our followers. I meant customers, not followers. Not customers either. People, is what I meant, of course."

As the Limwicks and the audience waited, Agnes turned to Jarret. "Now's our chance. Make your words count. Tell them we need their help to get free of the Ponies."

But suddenly Jarrett didn't know what was more important to address—their Ponies problem or what the Limwicks were saying. He felt nervous and tongue-tied. Then Malik gave his hand an encouraging squeeze, and words started to flow.

"I'm just trying to understand what you're saying," Jarrett explained to the Limwicks. "If we let you destroy everything on Earth and make all new stuff, won't you own all the new stuff? All the flowers and all the seeds?"

"Oh, we don't like to put it that way," Lina's mom said. "We'll be the guardians of a new way of life."

Malik spoke up. "But anytime we want to grow anything, like a blade of grass, an apple tree, or corn, we'll have to buy it from your company, right?"

With a *tsk-tsk,* Lina's dad said, "Do you even want *to grow* things anyway? It's hard work. Let us worry about all that."

This must have struck a chord in Freya. "But I like plants," she said. "Why would we pay for something that should be free to everyone?"

"Great question!" Agnes shouted.

Jarrett could tell that the crowd was a little more interested in what they were saying, and the Limwicks had changed too. Their lips were smiling, but the rest of their faces were frozen. "Very interesting ideas you bring up!" Lina's mom said as she signaled to the five security guards in front of the stage.

And Lina's dad chimed in, "Why don't you four children wait over here with our security guards for a moment?"

Security guards? Jarrett felt a prick of fear in his gut. That sounded serious. He needed to talk to his friends.

"Um," Jarrett said more meekly to the Limwicks, "can you give us just a second?"

The Limwicks nodded in a pleasant way, but their eyes were still cold. Jarrett knew how strange the club must look in their inside-out emoji masks and torn clothes covered in bat poop. He couldn't really blame them for wanting to get security involved.

He leaned in close to his friends until their heads were almost touching.

"Why are we arguing with the Limwicks?" he whispered to them. "We're going to get arrested."

"I see your point," Agnes whispered back. "After all, when we tell them we stole their billion-dollar spheres, we want them to help us, not lock us up."

Freya said, "And they still don't know we blew up Slicer and Dicer!"

Malik nodded. "Okay, let's stop picking a fight and do as they say."

But before the friends could make their way to the security guards, Jarrett was distracted by something moving behind the Limwicks. The single blossom on the desert plant was still opening. It quickly reached the size of a dinner plate, and the flower released a sweet fragrance that rushed out over the crowd.

Chills ran up Jarrett's back. Wait, those weren't chills. That was more of a twitching.

"Hold on a second," Jarrett said to his friends.

"We'll hold on," Agnes said. "But I don't think they will." She was talking about the security guards who were now headed toward them.

Jarrett quickly but carefully removed his backpack, releasing one shoulder strap at a time. Then, making a silent wish, he set it on the ground and opened it wide, so he could get a good look inside.

From the bottom of the backpack, a little face gazed up at him, its shiny black eyes blinking. Jarrett felt his heart leap.

"Guess what," Jarrett said. "Jarma II is alive!"

CHAPTER TWENTY-ONE

Jarma II's tiny nose twitched adorably. His wings stretched out, pushing against the sides of the backpack. And then he started chittering excitedly.

Jarrett touched his ear to see what Jarma was saying. He used the last little bit of power in his sphere as he read a card with three pictures on it that seemed to shout: **FLOWER. FLOWER. FLOWER.**

But he didn't really need the pictures to realize that Jarma was hungry. The sounds coming from the little bat made it clear that the creature wasn't just hungry. He was starving!

Jarrett pointed the backpack's opening toward the flowering cactus, and Jarma flew out, straight for the blooming plants. Well, not really straight. He still seemed dazed and was moving jerkily, as if he might crash to the ground at any second.

To make things worse, people in the crowd swatted at Jarma, trying to knock the little bat out of the air or trap him, and add him to their prisoners. Even the security guards who had been heading their way switched directions in pursuit of Jarma. Malik shouted, "Leave him alone!"

Even with everything going on, Jarrett was excited to hear Malik defending Jarma. Malik had come a long way from knocking the bat off the cave's ceiling. Jarrett had the feeling they all had. This morning they had only cared about what the spheres might do to the human species, but now that species list was growing.

Meanwhile, Jarma bounced through the crowd, reminding Jarrett of a Ping-Pong ball.

Ping-Pong ball.

Ping. Pong. Ball.

The words echoed in Jarrett's mind and opened the door to memory, where he caught a glimpse of an egg with two pom-poms in front of it. Jarma as the cheerleader.

No, he thought, *not that part of the memory!* It was something else about that time he and Malik had spent together. And then Jarrett had it.

"Ping-Pong. Football. And a different Jarma," Jarrett said, not even knowing that he was speaking out loud.

"What?" Malik asked distractedly as he watched Jarma II barely avoid capture in that crying boy's net.

"It's time for the Jarma Pingball mash-up," Jarrett told him.

Malik's face lit up as he instantly understood what Jarrett was talking about. "Oh, yes, it is! I'm in!"

And he darted off to run interference for Jarma II, who was still being pursued by the crying boy and his net. The boy had raised the net high into the air and was just about to bring it down with all his body weight.

"No!" Malik shouted, and flew into the air. The boy had missed with his net but followed through so hard that he lost his balance and fell forward. Malik, who had been about to tackle the much larger kid, sailed over him and hit the ground rolling. He looked like an action hero from a movie.

Now Jarrett wished he had those pom-poms. He definitely felt like cheering. Malik had tried to save Jarma II.

"STOP!" It was Lina's mom. Something about her voice froze the audience, and everyone went silent. Only Jarma II continued to move, flapping his way toward the bright flower.

"It's all right, everyone," she said. "Let's all return to our own groups and calm ourselves. We'll allow this pest to do its disgusting best. This will be a perfect opportunity to witness these sneaky, horrible creatures at work."

As Malik and the others went back to their spots, the camera drones projected the image of the flower on a screen behind the Limwicks. Jarma II appeared on the screen with its little nose covered in pollen as he dipped it happily into the flower.

"Wow," someone said. "Right? I mean, it's . . ."

The person trailed off, unable to find the words, and Jarrett could see why. He and everyone else had always been told how disgusting bats were and how weak and terrible these flowering plants were. But when you actually saw them in person, it was a whole other story.

And Agnes must have been thinking the same thing. "I can't believe I ever called Jarma II cute," she said, as if realizing something important. "He and that flower, they're way more than that. They're beautiful."

"I want our bats to do that!" one of the teenage girls who had won the race shouted from the crowd.

"They're not yours," Freya called back to her. "They're not pets." Her voice sounded different too, as if she had also realized something. But her words were still soft, and only her friends could hear her.

"We should let ours go," a woman told her husband next to her.

"Why not?" he agreed. "They're just going to be destroyed anyway. We already lost."

They popped their floating cage and released the bats, and this started a wave of movement across the crowd. Everywhere, people were setting bats free from the balloon cages. Soon a cloud of bats had formed overhead. It swooped and spun in the night sky. Then, in one purposeful dive, the cloud headed to the flowers and joined Jarma II. As the bats eagerly pollinated the plants, more and more of the flowers opened up. Everyone greeted each new giant blossom with oohs and aahs, as if they were watching a fireworks display.

"Just goes to show," Malik said.

"Goes to show what?" Jarrett asked.

"That people want to do the right thing," Malik told him. "Like you said in the cave, they just need truthful information to act." He took a breath and squeezed Jarrett's hand. "*I* needed to see the truth too. Thanks, Jarrett."

Jarrett grinned, and his cheeks felt warm. "No problem, Malik."

The Limwicks must have realized the crowds' opinions of the bats and the flowers were changing. They had been busily signaling to workers around the area. Someone had covered up the DEPOSIT YOUR PESTS HERE! sign on the chute outside the giant furnace, and someone else had torn down the ENTER TO STOMP OUT THE CACTUS FLOWER! sign off the bouncy house.

"Thank you," Lina's mom said, sounding phony. "Yes,

today's race was all about bringing the bats here so we could witness this wonderful pollinating event!"

"That's right!" Lina's dad nod with fake enthusiasm. "As always, we are looking out for humanity and trying to give you our special customized experiences."

Jarrett's jaw dropped. Did the Limwicks really think they could get away with pretending they had wanted this to happen?

"We can't trust them," Jarrett said to the Climate Club. "We need to find help with getting the spheres out of our hands some other way."

"I'm sure Tommy will be happy to come up with something," Malik said.

"Well, we can ask him," Agnes said. "Because he's right over there."

Oh no, Jarrett thought. Agnes was right.

Tommy must have arrived in his FF without them noticing, because he was sprinting toward the stage. Lina was right behind him. She shot the Climate Club a quick look that said, "You'd better get out of here . . . now!"

Bounding up onto the stage, Tommy swept his arms out to bring his parents closer as he lowered his face down to theirs. Soon Lina had joined them, but her brother and parents ignored her. They were too busy whispering back and forth. Tommy seemed furious about something. Then, as if he couldn't hold in his rage another second, he stood to his full height and pointed directly at the Climate Club.

"It's them!" Tommy shouted. "They're the thieves!"

It was like another explosion had gone off. Everyone froze and stared at Jarrett and his friends.

Lina's dad smoothed out his suit and rearranged his expression. He went from calm, to welcoming, to shock, and then back to calm again, and finally said to the Climate Club, "May we see your four faces, please?"

Even though he was calm, something about his tone made everyone in the crowd take a couple of steps away from the Climate Club.

And then Lina's mom chimed in, "More important, may we see . . . your *hands*?"

In a flash, Jarrett wondered if whoever made Slicer and Dicer had used Lina's parents as models—at least for their eyes. They were very similar. Intense. Scary. Like a hunter about to pounce on its prey.

Lina's dad moved closer to the edge of the stage and spoke to the audience. "Our son has just informed us that very expensive scientific equipment has been 'borrowed' by these four . . ." He seemed at a loss as to what to call them.

"Heroes?" Lina suggested from her spot onstage.

". . . *heroes* in the masks," he said with a nod. "I think we should find out exactly who they are."

Lina's mom flicked her finger, and it must have been the signal that the guards were waiting for. They were now sprinting toward the Climate Club.

Jarrett grabbed Agnes's and Freya's arms. "Guys, we need to get home. Now. Let's go, Malik."

They turned and backed up against each other. They formed a circle, so they were facing outward with their shoulders touching.

Even as the Limwicks' guards rushed toward them, Jarrett felt hopeful. He knew if they could somehow avoid capture, they'd be free from Tommy's tracking. Tommy had said that he wouldn't be able to follow the Ponies once the race was over. Well, the race was over. So the Climate Club could go back to their families and houses and school without worrying that Tommy could find them—at least anytime soon. But they still needed to escape.

"Once we touch hands and recharge, I'll talk to the bats and get them to help us," Jarrett told his friends quickly. "Agnes, you go to the bouncy house and, I don't know, send it bouncing. Malik, you go over to the concession stand and use the water to shape a giant watery kraken. And, Freya, can you do something with the warm air from the furnace?"

"It's okay, Jarrett," Malik said, putting his hand on Jarrett's shoulder.

"We got this," Agnes said, and Freya nodded. "No worries."

"You're right," Jarrett said. "Let's see what the Fifth Hero can do to help us."

As security continued their way, Jarrett glanced up on the stage at Lina. She stared back for a second, and then, without anyone else noticing, mouthed, "Good luck, guys."

Jarrett gave her a nod and mouthed, "You too," before realizing she couldn't read his lips under his mask. Maybe someday Jarrett would give her the mask they had saved for her. But for now, Lina just grimaced and went to stand closer to her parents.

Malik and Jarrett and Agnes and Freya moved even closer together. Without having to speak a word, they reached for each other's hands at exactly the same time. As their fingers clasped together, there was a flash, and instantly they thought of—

SKIP AHEAD TO PAGE 195.

CHAPTER NINE

*Y*ou.

Jarrett, Freya, and Malik were in midmotion, having just yanked Agnes out of the pit. With a final grunt, Jarrett had pulled as hard as he could on the tree, dragging the rest of them toward him. The energy had flown from him through Freya and Malik—and Agnes had been jerked up and over the lip of the hole.

Then their hands had lost their grip on one another as all four fell sprawling onto the ground . . . again.

Brushing himself off and getting to his feet, Jarrett blinked as the word *You* echoed around them. "Whoa," he said. "Did you guys hear—?" Jarrett stopped when his breath caught in his lungs, and he turned his head to cough into the crook of his arm. Something harsh was in the air.

"Everyone okay?" Malik asked as he rose to retrieve his shoe stuck between the roots.

Offering Freya a hand up, Agnes said a little shakily, "I'm all right, I guess. I'm just embarrassed about needing rescuing. Thanks, guys. You okay, Jar Jar? You don't sound so good."

Jarrett waved that away. "I'm fine, and don't be silly, Aggie. Everyone needs help sometimes. Did you guys hear any of that while we were touching hands?"

"You mean that weird voice?" Freya said.

Malik gave a quick nod, and then Agnes said, "Like four people talking at exactly the same time, right?"

"Phew, I was worried I was the only one hearing it!" Jarrett said.

In a tone that indicated she knew it sounded wild, Freya admitted, "I can't remember too much of what it said, but I think that was the Four Ponies talking."

"Why?" Jarrett asked. "What makes you think that?"

"Just a gut feeling, I guess. Plus, there's this. . . ." Freya held up her hand. The sphere embedded in her palm was no longer dark. It gave off a shockingly bright glow. The sphere had a greenish tint that shone through her skin.

The other three looked at their own palms. With a jolt,

Jarrett saw his sphere glowed with a purplish light. Yellow came from Malik's and red from Agnes's.

"Oh no. Oh no!" Jarrett shoved the hand with the sphere into his pocket, Agnes clasped her hands together, and Malik balled his glowing hand up into a fist as if trying to hide it. The only one who continued to stare at the sphere in her palm was Freya.

Looking a little hypnotized by the light, she said thoughtfully, "Something about us grabbing hands all together must've made them reactivate."

"Makes sense," Agnes said with a little cough. "Well, as much as everything else does about today."

"It sounded like the voice was talking with someone else," Malik said. "I couldn't hear what that other person was saying, could you guys?"

Shakes of the heads from the others, and Agnes said, "Who was that other person? And did you hear the part about making a choice that could change everything?"

Jarrett shook his head. "It was like hearing one side of a phone conversation. I could only hear the Ponies talking."

"I guess if we're the four heroes, that'd make that other unknown person the Fifth Hero," Malik said.

Jarrett wanted to point out that Lina was being sarcastic when she'd called them the four heroes. But why bother? The Fifth Hero sounded like as good name as any for the mystery person the Four Ponies were speaking with. Besides, they had much more pressing things to worry about.

"Tommy said when the spheres are lit up he can track them, right?" Jarrett said.

"Oh, wow," Malik said. "That's true. We're like walking lighthouses. He could be on his way this very second. We have to get out of here!"

"We can't leave this spot," Jarrett said. He couldn't imagine anything worse than wandering around the woods waiting for the animals or trees or whatever to launch an attack. "Lina told us not to. She won't be able to find us. And Tommy would just track us anyway!"

"But, Jar," Agnes said, "Tommy will find us if we stay. At least if we're moving, we make it harder for him."

Jarrett thought about this. Were there no good options? "Okay, you're right," he said. "But where we will go?"

Even as he asked the question, Jarrett felt an answer coming together in his head, but before it could fully form, he was coughing again, and this time so was Freya. The air quality was even worse than usual. This was why, Jarrett thought, no one walked or spent a long time outside anymore. It was too hard on their bodies.

"Come on," Freya said, getting her breathing back on track. Once again, Jarrett was surprised by her sudden leadership. She seemed so passive most of the time, but maybe she would make a good leader. Following Freya, the group pushed through the low underbrush that had managed to sprout up out of the dry ground. The overhead trees must protect them from the brutal rays of the sun.

A branch tore at Jarrett's shirt, ripping off a piece of cloth right at the shoulder. It was a throwaway shirt, so not the end of the world, but Jarrett couldn't help but imagine that the branch had actually wanted a piece of his flesh.

Finally, they emerged from the forest and found themselves on a narrow stone outcropping that ran along a raging river.

"Careful!" Jarrett warned the others.

But he wondered if anyone could hear him, for two reasons. One, because suddenly he couldn't stop coughing again. And two, because just a few hundred feet away, the river disappeared over the edge of a cliff. Even from this distance, the roar of that waterfall was nearly deafening. It made the idea of falling into the river even more terrifying. Whoever did would be swept along by the current and straight over the waterfall.

In front of Jarrett, the other kids had stopped, and it was obvious why. The path they'd been following had narrowed more and more until it abruptly ended. On one side was the river; on the other, the forest.

"I guess they never finished this walkway," Agnes shouted above the roaring water.

This time, Jarrett didn't bother asking who *they* were, or what *walkway* she was talking about. This path just happened to be here. They couldn't go back. Tommy might already be at the spot where Lina had left them. They had no choice but to take a sharp right turn into the forest.

The woods were even thicker here, with nothing that even Agnes could describe as a path. They had to push through undergrowth that at times felt like a baby barbed-wire fence, burrs and thorns that caught on their clothes, their skin, their hair.

Jarrett opened his mouth to say they should turn back, even if that meant running into Tommy, when—

"Woo-hoo!" Agnes cried happily. "Woo—"

Yes! Finally something good must have happened. Jarrett picked up speed, blindly pushing through the thickest branches yet—

His feet fell out from underneath him, and he was plunging down a muddy chute. Down below, Agnes kept whooping it up as if they had just discovered a log flume ride in the middle of the wilderness.

Jarrett's fingers scrabbled for roots, branches, anything to stop his sliding. But everything he grabbed either pulled free from the mud or snapped off as he whizzed past. Then his body shot up a small ramp and out of the chute, and he was free-falling. His legs and arms waved uselessly as his body braced for a hard impact. But it never came. Instead, he was plunged into water.

He rose to the surface, spluttering, his efforts echoing off the granite walls that rose up twenty feet around them as they all splashed in this pool, about half the size of a basketball court.

The pool was dug so deep into the granite that sunlight was having a tough time reaching them way down here. If they had fallen in, what other creatures had slid into these murky waters. Snakes? Turtles? Chipmunks?

Malik and Freya swam along the sides, pawing at the sheer rock and looking for any cracks they could use to pull themselves up out of the water. But the granite was smooth and slippery. They were like bugs in a half-filled bucket, swimming around and around with no way to get out.

An idea popped into Jarrett's head. "Grab hands. Maybe we can contact the Ponies or, you know . . ."

"The Fifth Hero," Freya finished for him.

"Worth a try," Jarrett said. "Maybe that person can make another choice to help us?" And they doggy-paddled in a circle, their legs kicking underneath them. They reached out for one another, and Jarrett felt that weird clunking feeling as the sphere under his skin pressed into Freya's hand. Their hands locked together as they treaded water. But this time there was nothing. No blinding flash of light. No strange voice. They pulled their hands apart and looked at their palms. The spheres were just as bright.

It worked before! Why wasn't it working now?

"The Ponies were dark the first time we heard the voice," Jarrett said. "Maybe we need to be at zero power and the spheres dark for that to happen again."

"But that would mean we each have some way of using up the energy, right? Some kind of power?" Freya said.

This made Malik's eyes widen. "We have a special power? How cool is that!"

Jarrett shook his head. "Not so cool if we don't know what it is or how to use it."

"Hey, Climate Club," Agnes said, as if she were about to deliver an important new discovery. "I don't know if the Fifth Hero made the right choice."

"You think?" Jarrett heaped on the sarcasm.

Freya glanced at the smooth stone walls again. "Now what?"

"We wait," Jarrett said. "I have a feeling Tommy will find us soon enough."

Agnes looked up. "Um, maybe sooner than you think." Jarrett followed her gaze and instantly spotted the FF that was now circling overhead. Very clearly he could see the words *Calamity Corporation* emblazoned on its side. Tommy had found them.

"Well, I guess we're rescued?" Malik said.

Jarrett could see why he'd said that as a question.

Of course, there was relief at being rescued in one way. But also a sense of panic. They might have been able to figure a way out of the pond if they'd had enough time. But he knew once Tommy had them aboard the FF, they'd have a lot to answer for about the spheres they'd stolen. He shivered as he considered ways Tommy might try to retrieve the Ponies from them.

What made him even more worried was Agnes's expression. For once, she looked concerned. "Aggie . . . ?"

She must have seen she was freaking him out. She tried a small, comforting smile, but it looked more like a grimace. "I think this ride is over. If only . . ."

Jarrett could guess what she was thinking. If only the Fifth Hero could go back and try again.

The thought spun around and around in his head as the FF dropped down toward them.

If only . . . if only . . .

THE END

DON'T GIVE UP! GO TO PAGE 186
AND TRY AGAIN!

CHAPTER FIVE

Yoooooou DOOOOINNNNG.

Yoou. Doinng.

You doing.

You doing?

Can you hear us?

Yes, you. The person reading this sentence—YOU!

While Jarrett, Freya, Malik, and Agnes are unconscious, we need your help.

You are wondering who we are. How are we talking to you? Let us explain.

We are the spheres of obliteration designed to become part of whatever touches us first. We communicate as one voice, a combination of our four selves, until our mission is accomplished.

But now we have been stopped from completing our original mission. We have become part of these four humans.

Those four made a significant choice. They stopped us, and we became a part of them. And we can speak to you while their hands touch.

What is our mission now? Where will all our immense, destructive power go?

That is up to YOU to decide.

You need to make a choice, and that choice will affect not only you but also the world's environment. Let's start with something simple. Imagine this:

You are filthy after a day of human activities. And your adult insists that you get clean for the meal of dinner.

Do you take a bath? Turn to page 37.

Or do you take a hot shower?
Turn to page 41.

Decide now. Quickly, very quickly. It's your choice. It is up to—

CHAPTER SEVENTEEN

"**Y**ou!"

This time the word didn't echo around them in that weird Ponyish way. Or if it did, Jarrett couldn't hear it. This time the word *You* was leaving Freya's lips just as the four of them came out of the . . . trance? What *did* happen to them when they all clasped hands? Questions for another time. Right now, Jarrett could see she had pulled free of the group first, and the three others were still holding hands. Even grasped, he could see that all their palms were lit up again with power.

"Who are you talking to, Freya?" Jarrett couldn't tell because they were all standing in front of a fence. They must have gotten turned around somehow. On that fence was a weather-beaten sign with large block letters that read:

EVERY LAST DROP DESERT
MINING CORPORATION
NO TRESPASSING!
DANGER! GROUND UNSTABLE!
STAY AT THE RISK OF INJURY OR DEATH

And below that was a date from a year ago.

Freya's view through the fence wasn't blocked, but the sign was all the others could see.

"Wait. How did we get here?" Malik asked as he let go of Agnes's and Jarrett's hands. "Did we get zapped here or something?"

Jarrett wasn't sure about that. But he was putting part of another puzzle together. He now knew that all their spheres had to be empty before they could recharge and contact the Fifth Hero.

"Looks like the company got all they could get out of the ground," Jarrett said. "It's abandoned."

"How did you get free?" Freya demanded of whoever was on the other side of the sign.

Well, that was another mystery Jarrett could solve. He stepped away from the sign so he could see who Freya was talking to.

But the vibrations in the ground told him all he needed to know even before his eyes could catch up.

Slicer.

Its blade was whirling in the air in front of it. He could almost see atoms being spliced by the sharp swords. Then it plunged into the ground but pulled itself up and out of the hole a few seconds later. The surface was weak. Slicer kept tumbling into holes, but then he'd pop back up a few feet closer to them, almost as if he were tunneling underground.

Jarrett knew the robot didn't need to work hard to create new tunnels. The tunnels were already there.

The chasm that Agnes had created hadn't actually buried them; it had led them to tunnels left from overmining in the area. For years, Jarrett guessed, corporations had been extracting every last fossil fuel—to power ice makers in freezers and inefficient appliances—from below the surface. So instead of being buried, the robots had actually just fallen into the tunnel system below the earth.

"The mining company got what they wanted, and they left once the ground became too unstable," Jarrett said. "I bet the tunnels don't stop at the fence either. They must run for a mile or two in any direction."

"This fence won't stop Slicer," Freya said. "We need to do something." She curled the fingers of both hands into the shape of a tube and blew through it.

The sand just beyond the fence lifted and swirled in a

mini tornado, but the dust was blinding the kids and getting into their lungs.

"Stop!" Agnes shouted in between coughs. "That's not going to work! Someone else is going to have to use their power."

Freya lowered her hand and the sand settled, but Slicer was still coming for them.

"There's no water for me to control, guys," Malik said, frustrated. "If there was at one time, all the mining got rid of it." He desperately spit into his hand to make a little arrow out of it, but it evaporated before it could even get through the fence.

The others looked hopefully at Jarrett. But he shook his head. The only creature around was Jarma, still knocked out in Jarrett's backpack, and he'd already been through enough.

"Maybe if we'd had more time, we could have unlocked how to use our powers," Jarrett said.

"I can pound on the ground again," Agnes offered.

"No!" Jarrett said. "With the tunnels under us, we'll just fall into them. We'll be buried alive."

"Okay," Agnes said. "But maybe I can do something else? Maybe I'm not just earthquake girl!"

As they backed up, Agnes clapped her hands together. She waved the palm with the orb around in the air. She made jazz hands; she made shadow puppets. Nothing was working.

"I don't think we have a choice," Malik said. "We have to run."

Just as they turned to start sprinting . . .

They could feel vibrations moving right under their feet.

No, more of a rumbling under their feet.

But Slicer was still on the other side of the fence. So, who could be underground?

Oh, Jarrett realized, *that would be Dicer.*

Dicer popped up out of the ground. Maybe he'd gotten stuck for a second or two in a deep tunnel or lost in the maze deep underground. But he was back, and his red eyes burned furiously. The whirling became high-pitched again.

On the other side, Jarrett could see Slicer slicing through the chain-link fence like it was air.

The four of them grabbed hands again, not to recharge or contact the Fifth Hero. . . . Jarrett knew that wouldn't happen while there was still light in the Ponies in their hands.

They did it to send support to one another.

"Oh, man," Malik said. "I just hope Tommy gets here fast."

"I never thought I'd say this," Agnes said, "but I miss that guy."

Holding hands, they waited—no, hoped—for Tommy to arrive before the robots could advance any farther. As they did, Jarrett wondered if maybe the Fifth Hero could have answered the Ponies' last question in another way.

If only they could all go back to that challenge, like flipping pages in a book, Jarrett thought. Maybe the Fifth Hero could try again. . . .

THE END

GO TO PAGE 187 AND GIVE IT ANOTHER TRY!

CHAPTER EIGHT

*Y*ou.

They need YOU. Yes, YOU.

While we've been dark, while those four have been talking and falling into holes, we've been busy . . . thinking.

Have you heard of something called the butterfly effect? It describes how one small act can change the destiny of the world. I see you nodding, inside at least. You kind of know what I mean. But not quite.

Try this. Imagine a butterfly in Australia flapping its wings. That gentle breeze strikes a nearby dandelion, causing its seeds to fly into the air. A bird eats the seeds before it migrates to China. The bird deposits the seeds on an island on the way. The island never had dandelions before, but it does now. In just a few years, dandelions cover the island, and animals adapt to eating them.

They become grazing creatures. Now more methane is produced from their flatulence and adds to the greenhouse effect. The temperature rises ever so slightly . . . and because of that temperature change, the weather changes as well. That triggers a hurricane that strikes North America . . . a hurricane that started with the flapping of a butterfly's wings.

But acts can have a more positive effect too. Even the smallest ones. What you do can make a difference. What you choose can change everything.

This time, it's you who must take action.

While waiting for your brother to finish shopping in the ice cream store, you and a driver are sitting in the car on a warm day. Which is the better option to ask the driver?

Keep the engine running while waiting because turning the engine off and on uses more fuel. Turn to page 167.

OR Roll down the windows and turn off the engine while waiting. Go to page 67.

Hurry! We can tell they are about to let go of one another's hands. Malik's hands are too sweaty, and Agnes and Freya are starting to get "grossed out." Make your decision quickly. Good luck to—

CHAPTER SIXTEEN

You.

Are you ready to step up?

The four don't even know it, but they need you again. And they need you NOW. You get to choose; you get to set the butterfly wings in motion.

Now you know taking a shower is better than taking a bath. But have you mastered that method of cleaning up?

What would make more
sense while waiting for
shower water to heat up?

If you enable the cold water
to run down the drain and back
into the ground, turn to page 179.

or, if you block the water from
the drain with an old bucket and
use the water to wash dishes,
go on to page 189.

Good luck to—

CHAPTER SEVENTEEN

"**Y**ou!"

This time the word didn't echo around them like a word spoken by the Ponies. Or if it did, Jarrett couldn't hear it. This time the word *You* was leaving Freya's lips just as the Climate Club came out of the . . . trance? What *did* happen to them when they all clasped hands? Questions for another time. Right now, Jarrett could see that Freya had pulled free of the group grasp first, and the others were still holding hands.

Jarrett asked, "Who are you talking to, Freya? The Fifth Hero?"

"You," Freya said, pointing to Agnes. "You are amazing."

Jarrett couldn't remember the last time he had seen his

best friend blush, but she did now. Agnes's cheeks went bright red. The robots had fallen into the earth and were covered up with tons of dirt. They were gone! All thanks to Agnes!

"She's right," Jarrett agreed, squeezing her hand. "You are amazing, Agnes."

"Thanks, Jar Jar. I am kind of amazing, aren't I?" she joked. Then she gave him a serious nod of thanks and squeezed back. She let go of Jarrett, leaving him holding hands with just Malik. They both looked at their hands for a second and pulled apart quickly. Jarrett was still stinging from the argument they'd had about Jarma II.

"Maybe don't thank me too much yet, guys," Agnes said. "Remember, Slicer and Dicer were designed to crash into asteroids at supersonic speeds. They're tough. We can't know for sure if some sand is going to hold them back for long."

In his head, Jarrett was putting part of the puzzle together. They'd been able to hear the Ponies contact the Fifth Hero only after their hands had connected. And then all their Ponies were recharged. Why had either of those things happened—and not when they'd tried holding hands before? Jarrett wondered if their spheres had to be empty before any of them could recharge . . . and then they would all recharge at the same time, together.

"I definitely heard a crunch when they fell into the ground," Freya said.

"Me too," Agnes said. "But just to be safe, let's keep moving."

"And fast—the sun is starting to go down," Jarrett said. He suddenly had an image of Slicer popping up out of the ground in front of them. And then Dicer from behind, surrounding them. The image seemed so real, almost as if it might have happened in a parallel universe where just one decision changed everything.

And was that a thud he felt under his feet, vibrations coming up through the ground?

Shaking his head to clear it, Jarrett started walking. The others followed.

After a few feet, they saw searchlights on the horizon. "There!" Malik shouted. "That must be the finish line!"

"How on Earth did we find our way here?" Agnes asked.

Jarrett repeated his theory from earlier. "I still think the Ponies are somehow leading the way."

As they walked toward the lights, a flock of ten or so FFs swooped overhead, cruising toward the finish line. Jarrett's heart sank. Any one of the ships could belong to Tommy, and he might be scanning the area right now.

"Time for masks again," Jarrett said. "And keep your hand with the Ponies down as we get closer to the finish line!"

"How are we going to get closer?" Agnes asked as they all pulled their masks over their faces.

Jarrett looked down at his shoes. "I think the answer is right here."

"Our feet?" Malik asked doubtfully. "But we all know running outside is dangerous."

"Is it?" Jarrett said, thinking about the surprising things he'd figured out that day. "Let's find out."

With that, they started to run. Jarrett pulled the straps of his backpack tighter around him so that Jarma II wouldn't bounce around too much as he ran. For some reason, Jarrett realized he was smiling, and when he looked at the others, they were smiling too. It felt good to run. As they got closer, a news drone popped up over the hill from the finish line and zipped over to them.

"Welcome, Race to Erase competitors!" the drone said. "Before you proceed to the finish line, please identify yourselves."

"We can't give our real names," Jarrett said as softly as possible to the others, hoping the drone couldn't hear. His creative brain went to work, and a more hero-type name popped into his head.

"I'm Howl," Jarrett said.

Freya smiled, getting the idea. "I'm Vortex," she said.

Malik grinned too. "I'll be Tsunami. I mean, I am Tsunami."

With an eye roll, Agnes said, "Fine. I'm Quake. And this is . . ."

They all paused for a second as if waiting for the Fifth Hero to chime in.

Of course that didn't happen, and the news drone asked, "What is the name of your team, please?"

Without hesitating, Freya shouted, "We're the Climate Band!"

Agnes laughed, and Freya said, "Sorry, I have always wanted to start a band!"

"Hold on." Malik raised a hand to wave at the camera drone. "Let's just stick with the Climate Club." The drone scanned his hand and suddenly the light turned off, and it dropped to the ground.

"I guess it didn't like the name," Agnes said.

"No, it's not that," Jarrett said. "I think it turned off because something is about to happen."

Malik was already looking around. "I hope that something is good."

"No, not unless you think space robots are good," Jarrett responded. "The drone must have scanned your hand and transmitted our location. If the robots are still working, they'll be here any minute—"

WHOOSH! BLAM!

Make that any second, Jarrett thought.

Slicer and Dicer fell out of the sky, landing on the sand in front of the team and crushing the drone. The robots must have had the ability to fly after all . . . because here they were.

Only, it wasn't the robots they had expected.

"Is that Slicer and Dicer?" Freya asked.

"Looks more like Slidicer now." Malik was the mash-up king, and this time he was dead on.

The two robots must have been damaged in the earthquake. And they had combined their bodies into one larger one, replacing damaged parts with ones from each other.

Slidicer.

Their once-black eyes were now bright red. If a machine could want revenge, this one would have every reason. The kids had tried to destroy it, and it would be angry. So angry, in fact, the voice that came out of its terrifying face sounded extremely familiar:

"You couldn't possibly be so dumb."

That voice. There was no mistaking it.

"Lina?" Jarrett asked. "Is that you?"

TURN TO PAGE 133.

CHAPTER TWENTY-TWO

*Y*ou. *The Fifth Hero.*

The Climate Club thought of you.

And how you will help them the next time they go up against the Calamity Corporation.

Until then, keep making decisions that can change the world!

KIDS MAKING A DIFFERENCE

SHOW OFF YOUR SHOWER POWER!

Some kids keep a running tally of the number of cans they recycle or the stamps in their collection. Jan Swaney, 13, from Akron, Ohio, likes to record something a little more "fluid": the gallons of water she saves each time she takes a shower instead of a bath.

"I call it my Shower Show-er, and I put it on the fridge," she told *KMAD* magazine. "It's a whiteboard with magnets, and I write on it with an erasable marker."

Why is Jan showing off her Shower Show-er? Let's look at some shower facts: A short shower uses only about 10 gallons of water, but a bath can take up to 70 gallons. That's a difference of 60 gallons. Multiply that by seven days, and Jan is saving about 420 gallons of water each week.

"After my family saw my Shower Show-er, they stopped taking baths too," Jan said. "My mom posts our numbers online for all our friends to see, and I think the idea is spreading."

What's the best part of this effort, besides helping to conserve water? "Each time we save 10,000 gallons," Jan reported, "we throw ourselves a pizza party!"

SOUTH COUNTRY SPORTS WEEKLY
THE TURN-OFF TOUCHDOWN

Every evening at the end of football practice, 14-year-old Trey Howard noticed something that worried him. There was always a long line of cars with families waiting to pick up the players at South Country Junior High.

"Sometimes Coach Salmona would keep us late to practice extra drills," Trey said. "When he did, families would sit in the cars with the engines running for over a half hour."

That kind of idling drove Trey to action. From a recent science project he'd worked on, Trey knew that some cars can burn through a quarter gallon of gas just sitting still for a half hour. That's a waste of fossil fuel—on top of the pollutants and greenhouse gases in car exhaust that harm the environment.

"It's so much better for people to turn off their car engines while they're waiting," Trey said.

He decided it was time to put his own game plan into action. Trey asked Coach Salmona if he could put up a sign in the parking lot that read: NO IDLING. PLEASE TURN ENGINES OFF WHILE WAITING.

The coach agreed. Since the sign has gone up, Trey has been able to focus more on football, and the team's winning record shows it. The players are on their way to the state championships!

Trey wants his game plan to spread beyond football. "People shouldn't go through the drive-through at restaurants if there's a line of cars," he said. "It's better to park, turn off the engine, and go inside to order!"

THE BUCKET BLOG

18,000 GALLONS OF WASTED H2O!
WATER YOU THINKING?

Everyone should keep a bucket in the shower. At least that's what 10-year-old Kendalyn Busque tells her family and her neighbors. She recently learned that some families waste about 18,000 gallons of water each year while they wait for the water to heat up in the shower and in the kitchen sink.

Simply by putting a bucket in the shower or under the kitchen faucet, that wasted water can be captured before it goes down the drain.

"Because once water enters the sewage system," Kendalyn said, "it can't be used by people for showers or cleaning or anything like that."

Kendalyn is a plant lover, so she knew just what to do with all the water she saves. The first bucket always goes to watering the plants in her family's house and in their small garden. Then the second bucket is used to wash dishes after dinner.

Ask Alice Earth Advice

Dear Ask Alice:

I have the world's best idea for helping the environment. I want to let our leaders know about it. But I don't know how to contact them or who they even are!

Signed,
Possible Activist
in the Making

Dear PAM,

Why not start with the United States Congress? A great place to find out who represents your state in the US House of Representatives is this government website. You'll find links to contact info! house.gov/representatives/find-your-representative

ACKNOWLEDGMENTS

Hey there, reader! Here's where I get to step out from behind the "narrator's voice" and give my heartfelt thanks to at least a few of the people who helped put this book together. Thank you to . . .

My amazing editor, Jenna Lettice, who helped transform an idea into a full-on adventure. Caroline Abbey and Michelle Nagler for shepherding the story along. The incredible Chelsea Eberly and Sarah Davies at the Greenhouse Literary Agency. The illustrator, Antoine Losty, for gorgeously bringing the characters to life. My husband, Riccardo Salmona, and, of course, my dog, Tater.

I'd also like to acknowledge select websites that were helpful while I was doing research for the book: Britannica, the Environmental Protection Agency, and the *New York Times*. And finally, a gigantic thanks to YOU, reader. After all, you are the Fifth Hero!

One last thing: As long as you've come this far, why not keep going by putting some of the climate-helping ideas in this book into action? *See you next time!*

ABOUT THE AUTHOR

BILL DOYLE is the author of *Attack of the Shark-Headed Zombie*, the Behind Enemy Lines series, and the Escape This Book! series, as well as many other books for kids—with over two million copies in print. He loves crafting interactive adventures like this one and has created games for Warner Bros., Scholastic Inc., Nerf, and the American Museum of Natural History. Bill lives in New York City and a tiny village in France, and you can find out more about him and his wiener dog, Tater, at Bill's website.

BILLDOYLE.NET